Praise for the *Ja...*

'This was a great find. A libr...
1960s England. Janie Juke, a... ...istic enthusiast,
is a very likeable protagonist. A real page turner. I've
already bought the next book in the series... hoping there
will be many more to come.'

'I got straight into the story ... I really like the way the
author depicted the 60s ...I felt as if I was there!'

'Intriguing detective story with lovely period setting and
interesting characters. I'm looking forward to seeing what
Janie Juke solves next.'

'Loved every page and didn't want to put it down. Can't
wait until the next one in the series.'

'Thoroughly enjoyable book. Kept me interested till the
end. Looking forward to the next one.'

'The glimpses into WW2 are particularly good. Solid
writing, great story, and Janie as a character is growing on
me. I hope there are more in the series.'

About the author

The setting for the *Janie Juke* mystery series is based on the area where Isabella was born and lived most of her life. When she thinks of Tamarisk Bay she pictures her birthplace in St Leonards-on-Sea, East Sussex and its surroundings.

Isabella rediscovered her love of writing fiction during two happy years working on and completing her MA in Professional Writing.

Aside from her love of words, Isabella has a love of all things caravan-like. She has enjoyed several years travelling in the UK and abroad. Now, Isabella and her husband run a small campsite in West Sussex.

Her faithful companion, Scottish terrier Hamish, is never far from her side.

Find out more about Isabella, her published books, as well as her forthcoming titles at: **www.isabellamuir.com** and follow Isabella on Twitter: **@SussexMysteries**

By the same author

**THE TAPESTRY BAG
LOST PROPERTY
IVORY VELLUM: A COLLECTION OF SHORT
STORIES**

THE INVISIBLE CASE

A Janie Juke mystery

Isabella Muir

To Mike
Best wishes
Isabella Muir
AUG 2018

Published in Great Britain
By Outset Publishing Ltd

First edition published June 2018

ISBN:1-872889-14-X
ISBN-13:978-1-872889-14-6

www.isabellamuir.com

Cover photo: by Marko Mudrinic on Unsplash

Cover design: by Christoffer Petersen

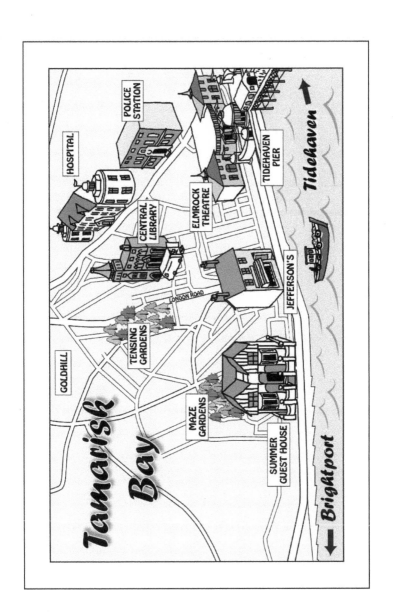

It's 1970 and Tamarisk Bay is preparing for its first Easter of the decade, while a certain family is preparing for a homecoming...

Chapter 1

Tuesday - Platform 18, Roma Termini

If it had been an ordinary day Jessica might have noticed the briefcase. Was it there, tucked under one arm, as he extended his other to shake her hand? Over the coming days she frequently reflected back to that moment, but all she could remember were the sights and sounds she was leaving behind.

The train for Paris was due to leave at noon. They both arrived early, with twenty minutes to spare before the start of their journey. It had been a while since she had seen Luigi and as he walked towards her on the station platform she was struck by his aquiline features, the way his hair fell forward over his eyes, despite him constantly brushing it back with his hands. He was maybe six inches taller than her so as he approached her she found herself looking up at him. His eyes weren't focused on her, they looked beyond her into the distance.

A porter walked behind Luigi, pushing a steel-framed trolley laden with luggage. Luigi held his hand up, indicating they had arrived at the right carriage. The porter unloaded two cases from the trolley, setting them beside Luigi's feet, then hovered, waiting for the inevitable tip. Luigi stuffed his hand in a trouser pocket, grabbing a handful of lire and thrust it at the man with the briefest of nods. Then Luigi turned towards Jessica. 'All your life in one suitcase and a small holdall?'

'Travelling light,' she replied, with a shrug and a girlish laugh.

'It's good to see you again. And thank you.'

'What for?'

'For letting me tag along.'

The cacophony of Italian voices meant they had to shout to be heard. Each of the thirty-two platforms at Roma Termini buzzed with comings and goings. Friends laughing as they ran along the platform, arm in arm. A husband hugging his wife before waving her off with a loud '*Ti amo*'. It was an orchestra of sound; trolley wheels that needed oiling, loud conversation, even music, all combining to make it difficult to pick out the tannoy announcement that the Paris train was preparing to leave. The language itself wasn't a problem for Jessica. She'd mastered more than the basics since she'd been living in Italy. But the announcer's voice was incoherent, muffled by the station's loudspeakers.

An elderly man tipped his hat to Jessica as he passed, on his way to join a queue at the mobile food and drink stands. Then she quickly moved to one side as a railway worker brushed past her with a broom in his hand. Not just noise, but movement all around her. Being a part of it made her heart race a little. It reminded her why she loved travelling, she had been still for too long.

'Having second thoughts about leaving?' Luigi moved past her to load his cases into the carriage.

'It's different for you, you were born here.'

'But you're going home, to your family.'

'Yes, and it's the right thing to do, but it doesn't mean I won't miss every bit of it.'

'The sunshine?'

'More than that, but yes, I'll be swapping a stroll by the port under an azure sky, for grey clouds and April showers.'

She stopped speaking to listen to an exchange between

two men, their voices gruff and forceful. One of the men raised his arms in the air, a conductor commanding his orchestra.

'The first time I watched two Italians having a conversation I thought they were arguing.' The memory made her smile. 'I was convinced they were about to start a fight in the street. Instead, it turned out they were discussing the best way to cook ravioli. It's their passion I'll miss, for food, wine, football...'

'Family?'

'Of course family.' One end of Jessica's scarf was caught by a gust of wind. She took the scarf off, rearranged it, then wrapped it around her neck again, tucking both ends into the collar of her blouse. 'Listen to me rambling on, just ignore me. Anything for the journey before we leave? Water, fruit?'

'No, nothing. Let's get settled.'

They moved along the corridor towards their compartment.

'I have 6D,' Luigi said, glancing at his ticket, before sliding open the door, pushing his cases ahead of him. His tall muscular frame made light work of lifting them both onto the luggage rack. He turned to Jessica. Her scarf was caught under the strap of her shoulder bag and she was struggling to untangle it. 'Let me help.'

'People will think I'm taking advantage.'

He raised an eyebrow.

'Young man, older woman,' she said. 'Anyway, I can manage, thanks.'

'Not so young. I'll be thirty next week.'

'Practically on your way to middle age,' she said and laughed.

They swapped seats so that she could sit beside the

window, but by the time the train pulled out of the station Luigi had turned to his newspaper, Jessica to her book. There was a long journey ahead.

A family of four joined the train at Bologna, bursting into their carriage with energy and noise. The Italian mother ushered her husband and two young sons into their seats, before sharing out several bags of food among them. They tucked into thick slices of Italian bread, interleaved with *mortadella*. She gave them each a tomato cut into pieces and Jessica watched as the children trickled its juice over the bread. There was an orange each to follow, expertly peeled, the fine spray of zest filling the air in the carriage with the aroma of the Mediterranean. As she breathed it in, Jessica thought of all the early mornings she had strolled through the fruit and vegetable markets, the stalls piled high with ripe peaches, golden apricots and juicy cherries. The smells would linger on her clothes, so that in the evening she would shake out a shawl or a scarf and enjoy the perfume all over again.

'Passaporti, passaporti.' The passport official made his way through the train several hours later as they approached the Italian-Swiss border.

Jessica ferreted in her bag and handed her passport to the thick set man, who looked uncomfortable in his uniform, the buttons a little too tight. His cap was perched so precariously on his head it seemed a jerk of the train would send it toppling. The official looked at Luigi's passport first, he had thrust it at him in an almost defiant manner.

'Now there's a man who looks distinctly disenchanted with his job,' Jessica whispered, once the official had left the compartment.

'We can't all love what we do.' Luigi turned back to his newspaper, holding it in such a way that the child sat beside him wouldn't disturb him each time he fidgeted. The boy, who was around seven or eight, was enamoured with a toy car. He spun the wheels, running it over the palm of his hand.

'What about you?' Jessica persisted, trying to strike up a conversation. 'Did you enjoy working for Mario?'

'Bar work is okay.'

'Plenty of tips? My bar work in Crete earned me more in tips than I got in wages.' Jessica held her hands out towards the little boy, pointing to the toy car. He handed it to her and she made a show of inspecting it before handing it back.

'Are you hoping to find work in England, Luigi?'

'Would it be easy?'

'Tamarisk Bay isn't unlike Anzio, a bit smaller maybe. At least that's how I remember it, but it's nine years since I lived there. There's usually plenty of seasonal work to be had and you're arriving at start of the season. But London isn't far away. I thought you might want to seek the bright lights of the city?'

'That's not why I'm going to England.' Luigi turned back to his newspaper.

'Did you see the way that man looked at us when we handed over our passports?'

'Disgruntled?'

'No, something else. Inquisitive maybe.'

Luigi shrugged. 'It's not unusual for friends to travel together. He seemed very interested in you. Perhaps he fancies himself an English wife?'

'Now you're teasing me.'

5

'You're still young enough not to be invisible.'
'Thanks, I think.'

It was early evening when the attendant pulled down the beds in each compartment. If Jessica had followed her brother into the army the bedding that was handed out might have reminded her of those days. There was little appeal in the solid pillows and rough grey blankets.

'Not exactly first class,' Jessica said, 'I've slept on beaches that were more comfortable.'

'You're too fussy, stretch out for a while, it doesn't matter if you don't sleep. Rest your eyes, at least.'

The family settled onto their bunks with little fuss. Perhaps they were frequent travellers, used to the transition from day to night in this little travelling hotel room. The father soon began to snore. The two boys top and tailed on one bunk, occasionally complained when one kicked the other. The mother had her back to Jessica and each time one of her sons moved she shushed them back to sleep.

Making as little noise as possible, Jessica eased the door open and stepped out into the corridor. Several passengers were standing, others were sitting on their cases, taking advantage of the cheaper tickets that offered a journey, but no seat. She had done the same thing in the past, to save money. She peered through the grimy windows at the jagged shapes of the mountains, made more eerie in the moonlight. In several hours the sun would rise and they would be beyond the Alps and heading for France.

In the corridor she slotted herself into a space between a young woman and a burly man. The man was resting his head against the window. The woman

6

reminded Jessica of herself years ago, when she first set off on her European adventure. Leaving Philip and Janie had been a wrench, but it was the right time for them and for her. Now she was heading back to them.

Once the dawn started to break, the milky light filled the carriage. The man beside her looked up from the window and turned his head from left to right, trying to ease out the stiffness in his neck. Jessica caught the gaze of the young woman and they both spoke simultaneously, causing a quiet laugh from each of them. The girl introduced herself as Cinzia, going on to explain she was travelling to England; it would be her first time outside Italy. Friends had told her it was bitterly cold in England and it rained every day. Jessica went to reassure her, but the door to the compartment slid open, interrupting their chatter.

'Breakfast?' Luigi asked.

'Good idea,' Jessica replied, 'but let me freshen up first.' Moving back into the compartment she took her holdall down from the luggage rack. The family had also started to stir, the children asking for food, the father grumbling that it was too early to be thinking of their stomachs. Jessica rifled through her holdall, pulling out her washbag and a sweater, before making her way to the small toilet at the end of the carriage. Once she had washed, brushed her teeth and put on a sweater, she studied herself in the small mirror above the washbasin. Sweeping her dark auburn waves away from her face she ran her fingers across the fine lines circling her eyes. She had always been freckly, but after nine years in southern climes the freckles had taken over. *'More speckled hen than elegant swan,'* she thought, laughing at her reflection. She applied a lick of mascara and a smear of lipstick. 'You'll do,' she said, stuffing everything back into her washbag and returning to the compartment.

The train seemed to speed up as they made their way along the corridor to the dining car. A couple of times Jessica bumped her shoulder against one of the compartments, feeling guilty in case she disturbed travellers who were still sleeping. With the blinds down on most of the doors and windows it was a guessing game as to whether the occupants were awake. As the train swayed around a tight bend Luigi, who was ahead of her, stumbled, brushing up against one of the doors. The blinds on the door were pulled up, revealing two travellers, a man and a woman, sitting opposite each other by the far window. The man's face with partly covered by his hat, which he had pulled forwards over his eyes, perhaps finding it more conducive to sleep. Luigi stopped so suddenly that Jessica walked into him.

'Watch out,' Jessica said, 'we nearly ended up on the floor.'

There was no reply, instead Luigi focused on the two people in the compartment.

'Move along, we're creating a hold up,' Jessica said, as two more passengers came along the corridor behind her.

A few minutes later they were seated in the dining car. There were three other tables in use, nevertheless the waiter seemed to be preoccupied with polishing the cutlery on the vacant tables. After a short wait he took their order and returned with a pot of freshly brewed coffee and a basket of warm croissants; the smells arriving at their table before the waiter placed them down in front of them.

Jessica broke the silence. 'You look as though you've seen a ghost.'

Luigi took a croissant from the basket and tore it into pieces, grabbing a paper serviette from the container in the centre of the table to wipe his hands. 'I thought I recognised the man in the compartment back there.'

'You should have said, we could have stopped. Catch him on the way back maybe.' She poured herself a coffee and offered the pot to Luigi. 'That's a coincidence, bumping into someone you know.'

'I'm probably imagining things.'

'I thought I was the one who hadn't slept.'

Luigi emptied his coffee cup and looked up, hoping to catch the attention of the waiter for a fresh pot. 'Have you told your family about me?'

'They know I'm bringing a friend.'

'What else do they know?'

'What else is there?'

The train swerved a little. The coffee slopped about, spilling into the saucers.

'Another croissant?' Jessica handed the basket to her companion.

'No, I've had enough. We should return to our carriage soon. I'm uncomfortable leaving our things unattended.'

'I wouldn't have thought anyone would be interested in my bits and pieces.' She drained the last remnants of coffee and pushed the cup away, mildly irritated by Luigi's fingers drumming on the tablecloth.

'Tell me again what your brother is like,' Luigi said.

'He's kind, clever and...'

'He's older than you, isn't he?'

'Yes, a few years.'

The finger drumming stopped for a moment, only to start again as he asked, 'Has his blindness changed him?'

9

'He's resilient, tenacious. It wasn't just the accident. He had to deal with his wife walking out and then having to look after Janie. He is a force to be reckoned with.'

'Sounds as though your memory of your brother is coloured?'

Jessica looked askance at Luigi, surprised by what sounded like an accusation.

'Rose-tinted is the phrase, isn't it?' he continued. 'A younger sister looking up to her big brother.'

'I lived with him for several years as an adult, there was nothing childlike about those times. He was a good man. He is a good man.'

'But it's years since you last saw him. He may have changed.'

'I know my brother. He won't have changed. Not in the way you are suggesting. Not for the worse. You're passing judgement when you don't know anything about my family and precious little about me.'

'I don't mean to offend you. It's just that there are layers to a person that can remain hidden. Their thoughts, their fears, their past.' Luigi shifted in his seat, looking around at the other people in the dining car, before refocusing on Jessica. 'And he fought in the war, in Italy? You said he was in Anzio for a time?'

'I don't think he fought. He drove trucks, ferrying goods around the place, vital supplies, that sort of thing. To be honest, it's not something he talks much about, so I don't know the details. But yes, he spent some time in Italy and he mentioned Anzio. It was fascinating to think he might have walked the same streets I walked. But back then it wasn't the Anzio you and I know. Anyway, you'll be able to ask him yourself soon enough. Don't be surprised though if he doesn't open up. People don't like to talk about their war experiences, I'm sure many of their memories must be impossible to cope with.'

She stood, taking her shoulder bag from the seat. 'I need to go back now, I've got a rotten headache. Lack of sleep, I suppose.'

As they made their way back to their compartment, the passport official pushed past them and on into the dining car.

'I'm surprised to see him still on board. I thought he hopped on, checked documents and got off again at the next station,' Jessica said, once the uniformed man moved away from them.

'Perhaps he's hungry,' Luigi replied wryly.

As they made their way along the corridor Jessica slowed, so this time Luigi almost bumped into her. 'This is your friend's compartment, isn't it? Looks like he's popped out,' she said, trying not to stare at the woman who was now on her own and looking mildly perturbed at the level of interest from two passing strangers. 'It's a shame you've missed a chance to speak to him, maybe drop back in a while and see if he's around.'

Luigi shrugged and continued walking, brushing past Jessica.

Once they were back in their own compartment, there was no sign of the Italian family, just a few crumbs left on one of the seats, leading Luigi and Jessica to assume they had got off at the last stop. The couchettes had been turned back into seats and the bedding collected.

'Ideal opportunity to rearrange my things.' Jessica said, pulling her suitcase from the luggage rack and opening it out on one of the seats. She smoothed out her clothes to make a fresh space for her washbag, which she had stuffed into the top of her holdall. She squashed it into one corner of her suitcase, closed the case and turned to Luigi. 'Give me a hand to lift it back up?'

As he raised the case above his head towards the rack, he paused, a frown creasing his forehead. 'Wait,' he said, putting the case back down onto the seat.

'What?'

They stood side by side, Luigi staring at the luggage rack and Jessica staring at his face, which was becoming paler by the second. For a moment she thought he might faint.

Then he grabbed the remaining luggage from the rack, thumping it down on the floor in an almost feverish panic. Each of them had brought coats that they had laid over the cases, but now he threw these onto the seat.

'What on earth is the matter?' she said, holding tight to her shoulder bag, fearing this would be the next thing he might want to grab.

He glared at her, banging a fist against the side of the train compartment.

'My briefcase, it's gone.' He stopped moving and stood with his arms outstretched as if pleading for someone to magic the situation away.

'What do you mean it's gone?'

'It's not there, Jessica. It's been stolen.'

Chapter 2

Wednesday - somewhere in France

Both passengers were oblivious to the noise of the train clattering along its tracks. Inside the train compartment there was complete silence, then Jessica spoke. 'Why would anyone want to steal your briefcase? There wasn't money in it, was there?'

'Of course not.' Luigi's face was flushed now, the paleness of shock replaced with something else. If someone had walked into the carriage at this point they might have thought they had stepped into the middle of a dreadful argument.

'I don't understand. Why would anyone want to steal a load of papers?'

He looked through her, as though she hadn't uttered a word.

'I must find the guard and report it,' he said, pushing her aside as he moved towards the door.

As he passed her she put a hand on his arm. 'Someone's picked it up by mistake. I expect it got caught up with that family's luggage. The ones who spent the night with us.'

'Yes, you're right, they've stolen my briefcase. We'll need to give the police a description.'

'A description? Heavens, Luigi, we are talking about a misunderstanding. I don't think we need to involve the police. I'm sure it was innocent enough. The children were clearly a handful, the poor mother probably asked them to help carry something and one of them picked up your briefcase by mistake. Perhaps he liked the look of it, thought it would make a nice school satchel.' She tried a half smile, but it fell from her face without him seeing it.

'This is no time for jokes.' His voice raised in pitch, drowning out the clatter of the train as it took a sharp bend.

'There's no need to shout.' She raised her voice to match his, but then in a more subdued tone, she added, 'calm yourself and let's take stock.'

'You English, you think everything can be fixed with a nice cup of tea.'

His eyes darted around the compartment as if the missing briefcase may suddenly appear. He stuffed his hand into his trouser pocket, removed a packet of cigarettes and lit one.

'You are letting the situation get the better of you.' She spoke slowly, as though she was a teacher in a classroom of unruly children. 'Sit down, calm down and I will fetch the guard.'

A few minutes later Jessica returned, accompanied by a tall, dark-haired man, in railway uniform. He wore steel-rimmed spectacles, which he removed, wiping them with a handkerchief before replacing them. The guard listened to Luigi's explanation, but seemed unperturbed.

'There was a family, we believe they've taken it,' Luigi said, taking long drags of his cigarette.

Jessica put her hand on his arm. 'By mistake, of course,' she added. 'We're not accusing anyone of anything. But my friend would like his briefcase back as soon as possible, as you can imagine.'

'And what was in the briefcase, *signore?*' The guard feigned interest, looking over Luigi's shoulder towards the window.

'That's no-one's business but mine,' Luigi snapped.

Jessica cast him a questioning look and then turned and smiled at the guard. 'Just personal papers, nothing of interest to anyone else, but important to my friend. I'm sure you understand?'

'*Si, signora,* I understand perfectly.' He removed his spectacles, breathed on them and then rubbed them with his fingers before replacing them. 'When we arrive at Paris we will file a report. You will leave your details with the French railway police and if, or when, the briefcase is found we will be able to return it to you. Soon you and your briefcase will be reunited.'

'That's not good enough,' Luigi said, his jaw tense. He threw the cigarette stub on the floor and ground it under his heel. 'We need to find the family. Can't you telephone the previous station, find out who they are, where they live? The passport official, he will know their names, he checked their passports during the night.'

The guard shrugged, adjusting his spectacles, which kept slipping down his nose. '*Scusi, signore*, but passports are checked to see if they are in order, names are not taken.'

Luigi tutted, glaring at the guard. 'He would have checked their tickets.'

'Tickets are checked, but names are not taken. If you look at your own tickets, *signore*, you will see there is no name, *davvero?*'

'We understand, of course we do,' Jessica said, glancing sideways at Luigi as she emphasised each word. 'Let's do as the guard is suggesting and wait until we arrive in Paris. If the family have the briefcase they will soon see it's not theirs. It won't take them long to realise their mistake. They are probably returning it to the station as we speak.'

'All the more reason to get on the phone right now...'
Luigi was pacing now within the limited space of the
compartment. The guard muttered something under his
breath as Luigi brushed against him.

'The passport man,' Luigi continued, 'he's still on the
train, we saw him just now. We can ask him what he
remembers.'

'You are mistaken, *signore*. The passport official left
the train at the last station.'

Jessica was tempted to argue the point, but instead she
remained silent.

The guard looked at his watch and then, as an
afterthought, he asked, 'Can I ask you why you did not
keep your briefcase with you when you visited the dining
car?'

'I didn't expect the train to be full of thieves and
villains,' Luigi said, glaring.

Hoping to calm an increasingly tense situation, Jessica
thanked the guard for his time, shook hands with him
and confirmed they would meet him on their arrival in
Paris. Once he had left, she slid the compartment door
closed and turned to Luigi.

'Are you going to tell me what has you so fired up? I
can't believe this is about a few papers and an old leather
briefcase.'

Luigi turned away from her to look out of the carriage
window. 'Forget about it.'

'I'm hardly going to do that, am I? You've made
enough of a fuss. I'm surprised you didn't pull the
emergency cord to stop the train in its tracks.'

'I thought about it,' his voice now almost a whisper.

They passed the rest of the train journey in virtual
silence. Occasionally Jessica commented on the scenery

as they passed through miles of French vineyards. The only response she got from Luigi was a nod, until eventually she stopped speaking. Instead she enjoyed an internal conversation that required no companion, just her own thoughts.

She almost wished the train would move more slowly, giving her longer to absorb the scenery. It was just a few weeks after her thirtieth birthday when she left Janie and Philip to make her first train journey down through France. She was so overwhelmed with the sheer expanse of the countryside that she spent the first few hours just gazing at it. She smiled at the memory. *'Thirty years old and as naive as a teenager,'* she mused to herself. Seeing it all again now gave her just the same pleasure. Carefully tended vines stretched out on either side of the train tracks. The patchwork of fields with overlapping shades of green and brown reminded her of the paintings she had marvelled over on her one and only visit to the Louvre.

As they travelled further north the weather closed in, reminding her of the endless grey of English winters. But she was returning in spring, her favourite season and looking forward to seeing daffodils and lush green lawns. If she'd missed anything over the last nine years, apart from family, it was the abundance of grass, in front and back gardens, parks and avenues. She promised herself the first chance she had she would take an early morning walk through Maze Gardens, kick off her shoes and feel the dewy softness of wet grass under her feet. Her brother would think she was crazy, but crazy was good.

After a few hours, the train pulled into Paris Gare de Lyon station. They lifted their cases and bags down from the luggage rack and eased forwards towards the exit. A porter came forward to help and he followed them and the guard to the railway police office. Neither Jessica, nor Luigi, had more than a few French words in their repertoire, perhaps the guard would act as their translator. The railway policeman was curt, almost monosyllabic, noting down names and addresses in a small black notebook.

'And the contents, *monsieur?*'

'Why is everyone so keen to know the contents?' As he spoke he threw his hands in the air, making Jessica take a step away from him. 'If it was a suitcase, would you want to know what was inside? Would you expect a lady to describe her garments, her underwear? Of course you wouldn't. It was a briefcase with personal papers, that should be enough. Besides, it's locked, so unless someone breaks the lock, they won't know what's inside, will they?'

'It's locked?' Jessica said.

The policeman looked from Jessica to Luigi, then back to Luigi again as he replied.

'I bought a briefcase with a key. Why wouldn't I use it?'

'And do you have the key?'

'Of course,' Luigi said, taking his wallet from the breast pocket of his jacket, holding the key out to show her. 'A key that is no use to me until I find the thief.'

'I wish you wouldn't keep talking about thieves and robbers. I'm certain it was a simple case of misunderstanding. A thoughtless moment.'

'There was a family,' Luigi said, ignoring Jessica's attempts to calm him. He described all he could recall about each member of the family he believed had walked away with his belongings.

18

When he had finished speaking, the policeman said, *'Merci, monsieur e madame.* We have all we need. We will be in touch with you at your address in...' he paused, struggling with the pronunciation.

'Tamarisk Bay,' Jessica enunciated the words clearly.

'Oui, Tamarisk Bay. *Allor, au revoir.'*

They were dismissed. Jessica thanked the Italian guard again, hanging behind, while Luigi stormed ahead towards the station foyer. The porter had been following them throughout, pushing the heavy metal trolley ahead of him. Now he was puffing a little as he tried to keep up with Luigi's long strides.

They had two hours to cross Paris, plenty of time, provided the taxi queue was not too long. The city centre was a mass of cars, buses and pedestrians, but after the chaos of Rome it seemed almost calm. The wide tree-lined avenues breathed space and tranquility. She watched as two elegantly dressed women sauntered past. Both wore tailored dresses. One had a cardigan over her shoulders, the wool so fine it was almost translucent. She noticed their cropped hairstyles and ran her hand through her hair, imagining briefly what it would be like to have it cut short. She shook the thought from her mind with a smile.

As the taxi arrived at Paris Gare du Nord, she took a little cotton purse from her bag. She had changed ten thousand lire into francs, which meant she could pay the taxi fare, leaving enough to buy a large bottle of water and two baguettes, each stuffed with Camembert.

'I'm not hungry,' Luigi said, as she handed one to him.

'Take it, you may be later.' He reminded her of a truculent child.

The train journey to Calais wouldn't take long and

then they would be on the ferry. Luigi had barely spoken since the incident with the briefcase. She had pretended not to notice, immersing herself in the book she had started when she left Rome. She had brought it with her when she left England nine years earlier and had read it so many times since then she almost knew it by heart. '*The Lord of the Rings*' was a tale of adventure, with young Frodo as fearless as she had been setting off on her travels. She smiled to herself thinking about all the terrifying ordeals that Frodo encountered on his journey across Middle Earth.

Once on the ferry they chose two reclining seats in one of the quieter parts of the ship. The last boat she had been on was a day trip to the Island of Ponza. She'd arrived on the island only to discover there was nothing to see but a beach. After a couple of hours sunbathing and swimming she took the *traghetto* back to Anzio. The little *traghetto* would have fitted twenty times over into this grand cross-channel ferry.

'Will you phone your brother when we reach Dover?' Luigi asked, bringing her thoughts back to the present moment.

'No, he knows we're arriving today, just not the exact time. I can't wait for you to meet him. He's very special to me.' An undercurrent of annoyance remained from their earlier conversation. She didn't need to defend her brother and yet...

'A brave man, or someone who accepts the turn of fate?' Luigi watched for her response.

'There's nothing wrong in accepting fate. We all do that in our own way.' They lapsed into silence again. When Luigi suggested he accompany her to England, she hadn't given it much thought. She was just as happy travelling alone, she'd had enough practice over the last nine years, but having someone to chat to along the way seemed like a fun idea. It was too late now to be having second thoughts.

The rough sea meant the cafeteria on the ferry was almost empty, most of the passengers struggling with the thought of food. The most popular items on board were the little paper bags considerately stacked around the ship for travellers of a delicate disposition.

Jessica laid back and closed her eyes, but then Luigi started groaning. She sat up to see that he was gripping the sides of the chair, beads of sweat appearing on his forehead.

'You're looking very pale,' she said. 'I think we'd better get you out in the fresh air.'

His lack of response and increasingly pallid skin told her what she needed to know. She grabbed his arm and pushed him ahead of her. 'This way,' she said, forcing open the door to the outer deck. A blast of chill air and sea spray hit them as they stepped outside, making them both grab hold of the rail to steady themselves.

'Fresh enough for you?' she shouted, her voice being carried away on the air.

'You go back inside, I'll be fine on my own,' he said, clinging to the outer railings, and peering over them at the seawater, its shades of gunmetal, topped with creamy white horses.

'Okay, I'll go back to the cases. I'll wait for you there.' After his explosion of temper over the loss of his briefcase he seemed to have little concern for the rest of his luggage. 'Come inside when you see the White Cliffs, you can't miss them,' she said, laughing.

Once inside she sat on one of the cases and took in

the scene around her. People swayed from left to right, struggling to stay upright and grabbing tight to any fixed surface. It was amusing to watch, she was lucky to have strong sea-legs. Perhaps she should have joined the navy.

Announcements over the ship's tannoy advised them of their arrival in the Port of Dover. Luigi rejoined her, his skin colour returned to its usual deep bronze. They made their way from the boat into the queue for passport checking, then out through customs. Within half an hour they were standing on the station platform. There were no porters in sight, no trolleys, no mobile food stands offering tempting snacks. Instead, halfway along the platform was the station buffet. She peered through the window, clouded with condensation on the inside.

'Tempted by a jam doughnut, or a nice cup of English tea?' she said, not expecting a response. 'It's one change at Ashford, then down to Tidehaven. Fingers crossed we'll get a taxi from there. The final leg of a journey is the worst.'

He raised an eyebrow. 'In what way?'

'We've travelled over a thousand miles in twenty-four hours and now it will feel like it takes us forever to go fifty miles along the coast.'

'Ah yes, I've heard about your British Rail.' He was looking down at his feet, scuffing one shoe along the platform.

'I'm being unfair.' She flicked her hair away from her face. A wind had picked up and was being funnelled along the platform. 'I wouldn't change it, for all its quirkiness.'

'Quirkiness?'

'Forget it, I'm rambling. I'm just saying it's good to be back. For all its faults England was where I was born, so it will always have a special place in my heart.'

He muttered something under his breath.

'What was that?' she said, as a train came into the opposite platform.

'Our homeland is always number one,' he said, raising his voice over the noise.

'I'm not sure about that.' If she had to create a pop chart of all her favourite places, the first Greek beach she slept on would have to hold a top spot. She smiled at the memory of arriving on Mykonos and finding all the accommodation full. She fell asleep on an empty beach and woke at dawn to find herself surrounded by other travellers. No tents, no sleeping bags, just a few essentials stuffed in a shoulder bag or rucksack. The simplicity of it was joyous.

Once on board their final train Luigi appeared to doze as they journeyed through Kent, the early spring rains creating a picture of lush greens and rich browns.

The Garden of England,' Jessica thought to herself.

After a short taxi ride from Tidehaven Railway Station, Jessica was standing in front of her childhood home.

'At last,' Luigi whispered to himself, as he helped unload the luggage.

'What's that?'

'It's been a long wait.'

'You mean a long journey?'

Luigi did not reply, as Jessica stepped forward to press the doorbell.

Chapter 3

Wednesday - the Chandler household, Tamarisk Bay

The notice on the front door announced that Philip Chandler's physiotherapy practice was closed for the Easter weekend. A chance for a well-earned rest. The last few weeks had been eventful with the birth of his first grandchild, then the christening, and now the imminent arrival of his sister and her friend.

Janie had prepared the two spare rooms months ago, anticipating her aunt's arrival in time for Christmas. The reasons for Jessica's delay were vague and Philip was philosophical about it, which did little to counter his daughter's disappointment.

'I thought she'd be here for Michelle's christening.'

'I think your daughter has enough doting onlookers.' The slight curl at either edge of Philip's mouth gave him away, despite his attempt at a stern voice. 'She's already got me, Phyllis and Greg's parents looking out for her. That's a lot to cope with when you're not even two months old.'

'Alright, you win,' Janie said, wrapping her arms around her dad.

'Truth is,' Philip continued, 'if you'd had the excitement of seeing Jessica in December, you wouldn't have it all to look forward to now, would you?'

'You should have been a politician, or a salesman. Although your positive powers of persuasion are not entirely wasted.'

'You mean I can persuade my patients to go forth and

heal themselves?'

Charlie's bark interrupted their conversation.

'They're here, dad. I'll let them in.' Janie pushed past Charlie, almost tripping herself up in her haste.

'Stunning,' Janie said, pulling her aunt close to her before pushing her away again to take a proper look. 'You look so...European. I'm not sure what it is, something about the way you have your hair, or maybe it's that beautiful silk scarf. Is it Italian?'

'How about letting your aunt through the door before you quiz her on every aspect of her wardrobe.' Philip waited for his sister to move towards him, holding his arms out. Instead she took both of his hands in hers, leaned forwards and kissed him on each cheek.

'My favourite brother,' she said, holding his face in her hands. 'And where's my bright-eyed teenage niece vanished to? Who is this beautiful grown-up with a pink bundle in her arms?'

'You're right about the grown-up part, being a mother certainly concentrates the mind. Not so sure about the rest. Bleary-eyed from lack of sleep might be a better description.'

'And your friend, is he here with you?' Philip asked.

Luigi stepped forward. He seemed unsure as to how to greet Philip and focused his gaze on Philip's face. 'Mr Chandler,' he said.

Janie was used to her father's blindness, but she could sense the discomfort of someone so fazed by it.

'Welcome to Tamarisk Bay, Luigi,' Philip said, 'let's go through to the sitting room. Janie, how about drinks for our visitors?'

The next hour was a flurry of chatter, with everyone talking at once, except for Luigi, who remained quiet.

25

'Phil, that beard makes you look quite distinguished, although I can see the odd grey hair.' Jessica ran her fingers over Philip's face.

'It makes life easier. Daily shaving can be tricky, even a little dangerous on occasion.'

'The grey hairs might be my fault,' Janie said. 'We've had a roller coaster time of it this past year, haven't we, dad?'

'Roller coaster rides must suit you,' Jessica said, 'It's not even two months since you gave birth and you look so laid back, like you've been a mum forever. Give the little one to me and let me take a proper look at her.' Jessica took Michelle in her arms and ran her fingers gently over her face. 'She's got your eyes and maybe your nose, although babies' noses are always just little buttons.' She touched the tip of Michelle's nose and she immediately responded with a little sneeze.

'Bless you,' Janie and Philip said in unison.

'But I'm guessing she has her dad's chin,' Jessica said, continuing to gaze at her great-niece.

'You're right about that, she's got Greg's dimple. He'll be chuffed you noticed it. He's such a star, he loves being a dad. He even helps me out with some of the night feeds.'

'Bottles then?'

'Absolutely.'

'Janie values her independence,' Philip said.

'Must take after her aunt,' Jessica said, laughing. 'When do I get to meet your star of a husband?'

'He'll be here soon, via a bath to wash off the brick dust.'

'Your husband is a builder?' It was only when Luigi spoke that they were all reminded there was a stranger in their midst.

'You must think us very rude,' Philip said. 'We've been chattering away and we haven't even asked you how your journey was. When did you set off?'

Philip wasn't able to see the shift in Luigi's expression as Jessica spoke. 'We had an unfortunate mishap during our journey.'

'I'm sorry to hear that.'

'Oh, it was something and nothing. I only mention it in case the railway police contact you.'

'The police?' Philip returned his coffee cup to the table.

'Somewhere on the train journey between Rome and Paris, Luigi lost his briefcase,' Jessica continued. 'We're hoping the railway police will retrieve it. And if they do, or rather when they do, we've given them this address. I hope you don't mind?'

'It didn't go missing, it was stolen.' Luigi's stern voice and even sterner expression seemed to be directed entirely at Jessica. 'There was a family who shared our carriage, they must have stolen it. The police have been unhelpful. They did not appreciate the seriousness.'

Jessica fiddled with the buttons on her cardigan, avoiding her friend's gaze. 'Come on, Luigi, we've been over this so many times. You don't know if it was that family and if it was then it would have been a misunderstanding.'

Although Philip couldn't see the glances being exchanged, he could sense the atmosphere, which had become decidedly chilled. 'I'm sure it will turn up and if it doesn't, you can always give Janie the challenge of tracking it down,' he said, trying to lighten the mood.

'Now you've got me intrigued,' Jessica said, grateful for

27

the change of subject.

'You'd best explain, princess. Otherwise your aunt will be imagining all sorts.'

'Okay, well the thing is, I've got a little sideline going.'

'Sounds like something a spiv would say in the war.' Jessica raised an eyebrow.

'I stumbled into it really...'

'Let me guess, it's to do with your passion for Agatha Christie.'

'How did you guess?'

'Let's just say I got to know my favourite niece pretty well over the years I watched you grow up.'

'Your only niece, you mean?'

'When I moved in you were five going on fifteen and when I moved out, well, you knew your own mind, even then. I remember all those times when you had your head stuck in an Agatha Christie book every time it was your turn to do the drying up.'

'It was always my turn,' Janie said, laughing.

'So am I right?'

'Pretty much, yes. I fell into it for one reason or another, but it turns out I'm good enough for someone to pay me for my trouble. Enough to treat Michelle to her beautiful *Silver Cross* pram.'

'We're talking private investigator?'

'Sort of. Although that sounds very official. More like a busybody on a mission. And yes, you're right. Agatha Christie is wholly to blame. In fact, Poirot more specifically.'

'What do you think of it all, Phil? I'm assuming Janie gave it all up when she was pregnant?' Jessica said, looking over at Michelle who had started to make grumbling noises that could easily have been mistaken for the cries of a kitten.

'Not a bit of it,' Philip said.

'So, I'll warn you,' Janie said, 'I can sniff out a mystery at ten paces, all I need is a hint.'

'Well, there are no hints forthcoming. At least not today,' Jessica said, passing Michelle back to Janie. 'Back you go to your mum, little one. I'm going to pop up and change, I've been in these clothes for forever. I'll leave you three to get to know each other.'

Luigi took the cigarettes from his jacket pocket and pulled out a miniature lighter that was tucked inside the packet. He looked over at Janie before lighting it. She got up and moved an ashtray from the sideboard, putting it on the table in front of him.

'We know a little of Jessica's travels, from her letters and postcards, but I get the sense her time in Italy has been special,' Philip said.

'There is nothing quite like Italian hospitality, but perhaps I am a little biased. It's a country that tugs at you, it's hard to leave, but I'm sure you know your sister is not a person to stay still for long.'

'She's been like that since a child. Always ready for the next adventure, short attention span. We were lucky she stayed with us for as long as she did. More than lucky, eternally grateful in truth.'

'Your accident must have been hard for you and for your daughter.'

Philip smiled, 'What doesn't kill you makes you stronger, that's what they say, isn't it? And I have Charlie here, to keep me in check.'

'And you, Mr Chandler? Have you travelled much?' There was nothing peaceful about the way Luigi smoked his cigarette, his face tensing with each breath.

'Please, call me Philip. The war took me overseas, but I don't count that as travelling. When Janie was a toddler we confined ourselves to days out and the occasional camping trip. When you live by the seaside every day can be a holiday. What about you, Luigi? Are you a city dweller?'

'I grew up in Anzio. It's where I met your sister. Jessica said you were there during the war.'

Philip stretched his hand down to stroke Charlie. 'My memories of Anzio are not all happy ones. The war destroyed many lives, and I don't just mean those who died. I try not to think about it too much these days. But I'm sure your hometown is a much happier place now.'

Janie watched her dad speaking, a dark shadow crossing his face as he spoke of the past. Luigi reached the end of his cigarette and stubbed it out in the ashtray. 'If you will excuse me, it's my turn to get changed. Which is my room?'

'I'll show you.' Janie plumped up a couple of cushions in one corner of the settee and rested Michelle against them. She gestured to Luigi to follow her upstairs, then, having left him to settle into his bedroom, she returned to the sitting room. Charlie had moved so that he was midway between Philip and Michelle. 'Poor Charlie, he's torn between guarding you or keeping an eye on the newest member of the family.' She lifted Michelle into her arms and touched her dad on the shoulder, 'I need to get Michelle's bottle ready, come through to the kitchen with me, dad.'

Once the kettle was on the gas, she turned to her dad again. 'Are you okay? I know you don't like having to dig up your wartime memories.'

'I'm fine. But I'm wondering about your aunt's friend. He's a very quiet young man.'

'Admit it, you're as intrigued as I am about him.'

'It must be difficult being launched into a family reunion when you're just an acquaintance.'

Janie moved towards her dad and put her hand on his shoulder. 'Now who's fishing? I thought I was the one to be intrigued by other people's relationships.'

'You must be your father's daughter then.'

'Point taken.' Having put Michelle's bottle to warm, she sat beside Philip, jiggling her daughter in an attempt to settle her cries. 'He's around ten years younger than Aunt Jessica.'

'I'm imagining a handsome Italian Romeo.'

'He's tall, lean and rugged and if you like rugged, then, yes, handsome I guess. He's got the most spectacular tan. No, that's not right, it's not a tan, he's more of a burnished bronze.'

'I think I've got the picture.'

'Will you give your granddaughter her bottle?' Janie passed Michelle to Philip and once Michelle was sucking contentedly she continued. 'He's a people watcher.'

'Interesting.'

'The whole time we're talking, he's watching our expressions, particularly you.'

'Maybe he's never met a blind man before.'

'It's more than that.'

Philip paused to move his arm slightly to support the baby's head. 'Sounds as if you've formed an early opinion of him.'

'It's only first impressions, I know, but there's something not completely straightforward about him.'

'Is that Poirot talking? Remember Luigi is your aunt's friend, so we need to give him some leeway.'

'I wonder if they are just friends, or something more.'

'I'm sure Jessica will tell us in her own good time.'

Janie stood and walked over to the window. The cloud cover cast a dull light over the back garden. She watched a blackbird hopping across the grass, before it flew onto a branch of the apple tree.

'We need to put more food out for the birds, dad. They're nesting, it won't be long before they'll need to feed their chicks. And water too, remind me and I'll find a bowl or something.'

'Janie, are you worried about Jessica? Do you think Luigi is a bad lot?'

'I can't put my finger on it for the moment. But don't worry, now she's home with us we can watch out for her.'

'She might not thank us for it. She's a grown up, she's led her own life for many years. It's not for us to interfere.'

'I know. Just ignore me. I'm seeing things that aren't there. Let me take Michelle from you now, she's finished guzzling.'

Jessica swept into the kitchen, her perfume arriving before her, halting their conversation. 'Now I feel human again. There you go,' she said, handing Philip a coffee percolator to examine.

Philip ran his hands over it, trying to distinguish its features. 'There's no cord or plug, so I'm guessing it's not electric.'

'No, it goes on the gas and a few minutes later you will taste the best cup of coffee you have ever had. I've brought a couple of packets of coffee too.'

She took the percolator from Philip, unscrewed it and

filled the bottom section with cold water. Having filled the little metal basket with ground coffee, she patted it down, screwed the parts together again and put it on the gas. 'I'm sorry about Luigi's outburst earlier.'

'You've got nothing to apologise for. Such a long journey would make anyone fractious.'

'It's not the journey so much, it's this business with the briefcase. He was like a man possessed when he discovered it was missing. I've never seen him like that, but it made me realise I know nothing about him. I'm not sure why I agreed to let him come with me. I didn't think much about it to be honest, but now I'm here and I've brought him into your home, into our family, well...'

'You worry too much.' Philip said. 'Oh, I can smell that coffee already. It's almost intoxicating.'

'You two go and sit and relax and I'll put a tray together. Do you know, if it's possible I'd say Charlie the 2nd is even more devoted to you than your first guide dog. He was such a sweetie, but you could tell that he'd rather be out in the garden playing ball with Janie.'

'He was a character, but this one is too, he's just a bit more serious, which suits me just fine, doesn't it, Charlie?'

'Well, if your master is happy, then so am I.' Jessica bent down and tousled the hair on Charlie's head, but his eyes never left his master. 'Janie, do you want to shout out to Luigi to join us?'

Leaving Michelle with Philip, Janie went into the hallway. She knew every rumble and creak of her childhood home, so when she heard the knocking sound that always came from the loose floorboard outside her father's bedroom, she hesitated on the bottom stair. A few moments later she heard the noise again. She tiptoed to the top of the staircase and saw Luigi coming out of her dad's bedroom. He had his back to her. She hovered on the stairs for a moment, waiting until she had seen him return to his own room. Another minute later she descended the stairs, calling out from the hallway, 'Luigi, we've made fresh coffee, we're in the sitting room when you're ready.'

Returning to the others she tried to put the incident to the back of her mind.

'Your aunt is really nice,' Greg said, when they were back home later that evening. 'She strikes me as a bit of a free spirit.'

'That's what travelling does for you, I suppose.'

'I wouldn't fancy it, all that moving around, chopping and changing jobs.'

The clean nappies needed folding, but instead Janie lifted each one from the laundry basket, shook it out and dropped it back into the pile, as if to fold it required too much concentration.

'Greg, something weird happened earlier. Before you arrived.'

'What?'

'I went upstairs to call Luigi for coffee and I saw him coming out of dad's bedroom.'

'You're kidding. Did you ask him what he was doing in there?'

'No, I didn't want him to know I'd seen him.'

'Maybe he wanted to borrow a tie,' Greg said, smirking.

'It's not funny. I don't like the thought of a stranger wandering about dad's house. We know nothing about him and it's not like dad can keep an eye on him. He could be a thief, or worse.'

'Don't start. I know all about your intuition, but this time it might be leading you down a blind alley. Speak to your aunt about it. Tell her what you saw and I'm sure she'll put your mind at rest.'

Chapter 4

Thursday - Summer Guest House

The next morning, Janie's mind was not at rest. Soon after breakfast she pushed the pram round to Philip's house. As she walked she mulled over Luigi's behaviour again, trying to decide how to frame the conversation she planned to have with her aunt, with her dad out of earshot.

Luck was on her side. She arrived to discover Philip out, giving Charlie his morning walk. Jessica was washing up, her hands full of suds.

'Good timing, you've given me the excuse I needed to stop,' she said, drying her hands.

'We should come straight out and ask him what he was doing.' Jessica said, once Janie had explained her concerns to her. 'Why would he be nosing in your dad's room? I'll admit he's been a bit fixated about meeting Phil, asking me questions about his time in the war. Then your dad offers him hospitality and he repays him by snooping. I'm going to say something to him. I'll admit I hate confrontation, but the more time I spend with him, the more I doubt him.'

'Don't worry, I've had an idea. Let's see if Rosetta has a room free.'

'Rosetta?'

'She's lovely and she's Italian. It couldn't be more perfect. She runs a little guest house down on the seafront.'

'You sure we're not just moving the problem onto Rosetta? It hardly seems fair. And how are we going to justify kicking him out after just one night?'

'We can explain that the room we've put him is so tiny and was only ever intended as a quick stop gap for his first night, which is true. It's been dad's box room for years. I stuffed everything up in the loft when we found out you were bringing a friend. Anyway, when he discovers the *Summer Guest House* is run by someone from his home country I'll bet he'll jump at the chance. And don't worry about Rosetta, she'll keep him in check.'

Jessica smiled. 'Do you approach everything with such positivity?' Then, hearing the front door open and the sound of Charlie's feet approaching, she quickly added, 'One thing you haven't thought about is money.'

'How do you mean?'

'I'm guessing Rosetta doesn't let her rooms for free, out of the goodness of her heart?'

'Good point. But she'll give us the best deal, I'm sure. Anyway, Luigi won't have expected to stay here for nothing, would he?' Janie tried to read the expression on her aunt's face, but failed. 'I'll tell him if you like, it might be better coming from me.'

A slightly awkward conversation and a phone call later, resulted in Janie leading Luigi along the seafront to the *Summer Guest House*. Just as Rosetta Summer finished vacuuming the guest bedrooms, the front doorbell rang. By the time she had run down the three flights of stairs and made her way into the hall, it rang again.

'*Aspetta, vengo*. I'm coming,' she called out, brushing a stray hair from her face.

'Rosetta, this is Luigi,' Janie said, nudging him forwards into the hallway. 'Sorry, we're a bit early. It's just that I need to get straight back to Michelle. I've left her at dad's.'

'Come in. *Piacere*, it's very nice to meet you. Someone from home to talk to, very wonderful.'

Luigi stepped forward, holding out his hand. 'Thank you, Signora Summer, but we are in England. We should speak English, don't you think?'

Janie raised an eyebrow, noticing Rosetta's smile fade. 'We're grateful you have a room free. Being Easter, I wasn't sure how busy you'd be.'

Tamarisk Bay had long been a holiday destination for people making the short journey from London and its surroundings. Visitors were attracted to the long promenade and open-air bathing pool and several new cafés and restaurants had opened up recently, creating a real buzz about the place.

Summer Guest House was at the western end of the seafront in Tamarisk Bay. Built around the turn of the century its red brick facade gave it a homely appearance, although much of the wooden paintwork was suffering as a result of the sea air that blasted through, regardless of the season. For the last few years Rosetta had taken in long-term lodgers, but this year she had decided to take advantage of the growing tourist trade.

The inside of the guest house was just as homely, despite its tired decorations. All the rooms would have benefitted from a fresh coat of paint, but that meant spending money that Rosetta didn't have.

Rosetta gestured to them to follow her into the amply-sized dining room, which was sandwiched between the sitting room at the front of the house and the kitchen in the rear. The only windows in the dining room looked towards the east, over a little strip of land that lay between Rosetta and her neighbour. It seemed as though no-one owned this piece of wasteland, which was a tumble of weeds and brambles. As if to compensate, the dining room wallpaper was a colourful pattern of large and small bouquets of cut flowers and any thoughts of tired paintwork were soon forgotten. The design brought such gaiety to the room it felt like walking into a flower shop.

'I will show your friend to his room and then we can complete the paperwork once he has unpacked.' Rosetta's voice and manner were now brisk and businesslike.

'Paperwork?' The note of alarm in Luigi's voice made both women exchange a look.

'I need your passport, just to take a few details,' Rosetta explained.

'There was an unfortunate incident during his train journey from Italy. Luigi lost his briefcase.' Janie hoped her explanation might defuse the tension she detected from her aunt's travelling companion.

'Oh, I am sorry. But you have your passport?'

'Yes, here,' he said, thrusting the passport at Rosetta.

'I just need to complete my guest register.' She hesitated and looked up at Luigi. 'You are Luigi Denaro?'

'Yes.'

She handed the passport back to him. 'I will take you to your room now. It is on the second floor, the bathroom on the left, your room on the right. Number two on the door. Please, make yourself comfortable. Supper is at six.'

Janie waited in the hallway until Rosetta returned.

'He is a friend of your auntie?' Rosetta said quietly.

'More of an acquaintance. He's a bit of a strange one though. I can't make him out, he's hardly got a word to say. I'm not sure why he's come to England, but he doesn't seem thrilled about being here.'

Janie's mind flashed back to the night before when she had seen Luigi coming out of her dad's bedroom. 'You don't know him, do you? You seemed to recognise his name.'

'The name Denaro. I remember it from somewhere. No matter.' Rosetta's concentration appeared to drift for a moment as though her thoughts were elsewhere. Then she smiled. 'Perhaps he will relax a little more now he is with me. A reminder of home for him, eh? And tomorrow I have another visitor arriving from Italy.'

'A friend of yours?'

'No, I think he is a businessman.'

'What's an Italian businessman doing here in Tamarisk Bay? Perhaps he wants to start up a new coffee shop? Competition for *Jefferson's*, I'd better tell Richie to watch out.' Janie smiled.

'All I know is his name, Mr Bertrand Williams.'

'He sounds English, maybe he's got family locally. Although it's not a name I recognise from Tamarisk Bay. Mind you, I did go to school with a Margaret Williams.' Janie chattered on without realising that Rosetta was barely listening.

'I am pleased you come here today. I have an idea. Tomorrow is Good Friday. I would like to cook a special meal and I would like to meet your aunt. Will you come? You, Greg, your father? Bring the baby too. I haven't seen her for over a week and at this age they change every day.'

'Are you sure? That's a lot of cooking. Why don't we each bring a dish?'

'It must be fish. All fish on Good Friday. I will cook.'

'Okay, I'll tell the others.'

'Ask Libby and her grandmother as well.'

'Okay, but now I must get my skates on, or I'll be in serious trouble. What about your in-laws? Will they come over from Tidehaven?'

'No, they are too frail to go out in the evening. I will go to see them on Easter Sunday, after I have done the breakfast for my guests.'

'It's a shame you don't have any family here.' Janie touched Rosetta's shoulder in a gesture of comfort, but the Italian pulled away.

'I have friends,' she said, forcing her face into a smile.

'Okay, tomorrow then. What time?'

'6.30.'

'6.30 it is.'

'I'd better run or Michelle will be screaming for her next bottle.'

Up in Room 2 Luigi opened his suitcases. One case contained every sweater he owned. Already since his arrival here in England he was feeling in need of extra layers. His second suitcase was part filled with cigarettes. He guessed it would be difficult to find his favourite brand here in Tamarisk Bay, so he had come well prepared.

He'd had his first cigarette when, at the age of fifteen, he was left in the house on his own for a weekend. His father was away on business, as usual, and his mother had made a trip to Bologna. It was rare for his mother to go anywhere outside their home town of Anzio. Occasionally she would spend a day in Rome, returning with a new pair of shoes or a handbag. She'd told him the Bologna trip was to a dressmaker who had been recommended to her by a friend. He remembered how she was like a young girl going to her first party, full of anticipation. It was a mystery to him how anyone could get so excited by clothes. To him they were merely something that had to be kept clean and neatly pressed, an annoyance if anything.

Before she left for her weekend of fashion she showed him every item of food in the fridge and cupboards. Opening each door, she spelled out what she had prepared for each meal in such a painstaking way he vowed to himself to spend the whole weekend out of the house. She would return to find all the food untouched. It was a small act of rebellion.

As soon as she left he went into his parents' bedroom. He couldn't remember the last time he had been in there. When he was a toddler perhaps. He opened the wardrobes. His father's was filled with suits, neatly ordered, with shoes lined up in pairs below. As he opened his mother's wardrobe waves of her perfume washed over him. He stepped back, struck by a sense of her presence, when in reality it was merely her scent. Next he sat at her dressing table, opening up the jewellery and trinket boxes that covered the surface. He recognised the double string of pearls, a recent gift from his father. She had unwrapped the gift in front of Luigi and asked him to help fasten the clasp. There were matching earrings too. They were the latest offering of many. Each time his father returned from a business trip he would bring a gift. Perfume sometimes, occasionally flowers, but often jewellery. And yet now, as he looked through her jewellery he realised she had taken none of it with her on her shopping trip.

Moving away from his mother's dressing table he walked past the bed. Unlike his own, which was topped with a single linen coverlet, theirs was covered with a sumptuous satin bedspread and piled high with silk cushions. Either side of the bed stood rosewood bedside cabinets. He pulled open one of the drawers, not knowing whether it was his mother's or father's side of the bed. But once he opened it he knew. There, in amongst a leather wallet, pencils, and bizarrely a silver whistle, lay a packet of cigarettes. He had never seen his mother smoke, but he had rarely seen his father without a cigarette in his hand. This then was the best act of rebellion. He picked up the packet, pulled out a cigarette and put it in his mouth, enjoying the feel of it. He pushed his hand towards the back of the drawer and discovered a lighter. He held the lighter for a moment, admiring it. The body of the lighter was the palest green, onyx perhaps, the top and mechanism fashioned from silver. He flicked it, the flint firing into action, providing a bright little flame. He lit the cigarette and drew in a long breath.

Now, fifteen years later, standing in Room 2 in the *Summer Guest House*, he repeated the same action and it felt good.

Chapter 5

Good Friday - Summer Guest House

When the Chandlers and Jukes walked into the guest house the next evening the aromas wafting through from Rosetta's kitchen would have enticed even the most abstemious dieter. 'Smells like a feast.' Janie planted a shopping bag down on the kitchen counter, before unpacking the contents.

'I just do a few things, some pasta...'

'Garlic, tomato and...what else can I smell?'

'*Cozze*. Mussels. Fresh from the fishermen today.'

'Tamarisk Bay mussels *alla Rosetta*? Sounds delicious. We've brought beers and chocolates, shall I put them in the fridge?'

'*Si*. Go through, sit down. Where is the baby?'

'We've left Michelle with my parents for the evening,' Greg said. 'Mum can't get enough of her. Trouble is she sleeps most of the time, so I wouldn't be surprised if they poke her to wake her up, just so they get a cuddle.'

Summer Guest House was a little grander than Janie's childhood home, but not in an ostentatious way. Ornate cornices and decorative ceiling roses in Rosetta's dining room held a fascination for Janie, as did the display cabinet that rose almost to ceiling height, filling the alcove to one side of the chimney breast. The first time Janie had seen the collection of china and porcelain teapots of every colour and shape she complimented Rosetta on it, but it was only later it struck her as an unlikely choice of chinaware for an Italian to collect, particularly one who couldn't bear to drink tea. She asked

44

Rosetta about it one day and was told that the teapots had been passed down to her husband from his grandmother.

'They remind me of my husband,' she said, 'although he couldn't stand them. *What's the point of having so many teapots,* he would say, *you only need one for a good strong cuppa.'* When she spoke of her husband she would try to alter her voice to emulate her memory of his, dropping it to a deep, throaty growl, which made Janie smile.

The guests settled themselves around the table, leaving two chairs empty for Rosetta's latest guests, Luigi and Bertrand Williams. Charlie had nestled under Philip's chair, resting his head on his master's feet, with his nose twitching for any crumb or morsel that might descend from the table above. Drinks were poured and the chatter was lively. Rosetta trotted back and forth from the kitchen bringing various dishes until the table was covered, barely leaving space for the water jug.

Janie gazed around, taking in a sense of old-fashioned grandeur. The mahogany table was covered with a heavy damask tablecloth, laid with neatly polished glass and cutlery.

She had only been in one other guest house in her life. She and Greg had spent their first two nights as a newly married couple just outside Brighton, in a place grandly described in the advert as a 'country house hotel'. But in truth *Twilight B&B* was nothing more than a bed and breakfast, albeit a nice one. The newlyweds were allocated the best table at breakfast, set in the bay window, with the only other couple staying there taking the table nearest to the serving hatch, where the kitchen aromas drifted through. Each of the tables were laid for just two people and she wondered what might happen if a family came to stay.   White linen tablecloths covered the small tables in *Twilight B&B*, and the blue and white crockery was sturdy and functional. On the sideboard the selection of breakfast fare didn't extend beyond cornflakes and Weetabix. There was always such a hush about the place that when Greg whispered to her to pass the ketchup all she wanted to do was giggle.

Rosetta, by contrast, had achieved an air of relaxed elegance in her dining room.   A lace runner adorned the top of the walnut sideboard, where a crystal glass fruit bowl took centre stage, piled high with oranges and apples. Smaller glass bowls contained walnuts and almonds, still in their shells, with a pair of ornate nutcrackers laying on top. It was as though Rosetta was trying to create the abundance of her homeland here in Tamarisk Bay.

'These olives, and the breadsticks, where do you find all these goodies? You must have a secret store,' Jessica said. 'I've only been home a couple of days and I'm already missing Italian food, I had no idea you could buy it locally.'

'There is a shop in Little Italy, it is like walking back into my favourite village shop in Puglia.'

'Little Italy?' Jessica slid a selection of olives onto her plate, smiling as Janie bit into one and pulled a face.

'In London, the Italian quarter.' Rosetta's expression was wistful. 'It's wonderful, you should go there one day.'

'Have you been up to London recently?' Janie asked.

Rosetta paused before replying, lifting the water jug and refilling the glasses. 'I go when I can,' she said, avoiding Janie's gaze.

'Let's hope Libby's *other engagement* is worth her missing out on all these flavours of Italy,' Janie said.

'She had a date?' Rosetta asked.

'Ray and Libby are pretty much inseparable. She keeps saying how much she wants to go to Italy and now she's missed the chance for vital research. What's your new arrival like, Rosetta? Mr Williams, isn't it?'

'He seems nice,' Rosetta replied. 'As you would imagine an English businessman to be, very proper, with his serious face and his pipe.'

'That sounds so funny when you say it,' Janie said.

Rosetta fiddled with the string of amber beads around her neck before continuing. 'And your friend, he knows him.' She directed her comment at Jessica.

'Luigi knows him?' Jessica asked.

'*Si.*' Rosetta stood up, refilled her own glass with water, then sat again.

'That's a weird coincidence,' Greg said, looking at Rosetta for more of an explanation.

'When Mr Williams arrived this morning, Mr Denaro was coming out of the breakfast room. They met each other in the hall and spoke together.'

'If Luigi knew he had come from Italy, he would have offered a welcome.' Philip said.

'No, Mr Denaro was unhappy. He said some words to Mr Williams and his face was dark.'

'What do you mean, Rosetta?' Janie asked.

'I only know what I see, what I hear. He was angry.' When Rosetta was irritated her voice tended to rise in pitch, which it did now.

'We're not doubting you. It just seems odd,' Janie said.

'Maybe I know this Mr Williams,' Jessica said. 'It's funny, because Luigi thought he recognised someone on the train from Rome. Now that would be a small world, if the same man has turned up here.'

Rosetta tutted, but said no more, returning to the kitchen, to appear at the table again with yet more dishes of olives. Italian music was playing in the background and Jessica started humming to one of the tunes. 'Oh, this is one of my favourites. They played it all the time in the bar where Luigi worked.'

'A bit different from your past musical tastes.' Philip quipped. 'I remember when you first came to stay with us you played Bill Haley's *Rock Around the Clock* on repeat until it nearly drove me mad.'

'What about you and your Frank Sinatra?' Jess replied. 'Poor Janie didn't stand a chance. Do you remember when she asked us to buy her that Rosemary Clooney record? What was it called?'

'*Mambo Italiano*. I remember hearing it on dad's radio and jigging around to it. I can't have been more than nine or ten years old,' Janie said, closing her eyes in an attempt to remember the first bars of the song.

'An early starter,' Philip said, laughing.

'I wonder where the other guests are? We should start to eat, or the food will spoil.' Jessica stood and moved to the end of the table. 'I'll go and chase them up. You know what men can be like, they have no sense of what goes into preparing a meal like this.'

'No, I will go.' There was still a touch of irritation in Rosetta's voice.

Each person around Rosetta's table that evening had their own memory of the next few minutes.

Jessica was certain that a minute passed, maybe two, before a piercing scream that instantly destroyed the conviviality of the evening.

Try as he might, Greg recalled little except for Charlie's barking, that almost drowned out the scream.

Janie found it useful to close her eyes when trying to refocus on a past event, Philip, on the other hand, didn't need to close his eyes. All the information he needed came to him through his hearing and an ability he had developed to sense movement. Perhaps it was the subtle changes in the air around him, or vibrations, but whatever it was he knew that for those first couple of seconds after Rosetta screamed each of her guests remained absolutely still. And silent.

Janie was the first to move. She ran out into the hallway, calling Rosetta's name.

'What is it? Are you okay?'

Not waiting for a response, she ran up the three flights of stairs to the guest bedrooms. Jessica stood at the foot of the stairs, while Philip tried to pacify Charlie. For the next few minutes Philip heard only muffled voices, footsteps and someone crying. He felt Greg's hand on his shoulder as the second scream came, not as loud as the first, but somehow more chilling. Then he recognised his daughter's footsteps as she came back into the kitchen.

'What is it, Janie?'

'Dad.' As she held his hand he sensed her trembling. 'It's something dreadful.'

'Talk to me, tell me what's happened.'

'It's Mr Williams. He's dead. He's just laying there on his bed, dead.'

Chapter 6

Good Friday - Summer Guest House

When Janie reached the landing, Rosetta was standing in the bedroom doorway of Room 3, her hands covering her face. She looked like a marble statue, her skin pale and no suggestion of breath. As Janie approached, she let out a second scream, but this time the pitch was lower, as though she had exhausted her emotions. Janie felt Rosetta trembling as she put her arms around her.

'Ssh now, it's alright.' As Janie spoke she looked beyond Rosetta into the bedroom of the man who had held up supper. Mr Williams was laying on his bed, fully dressed and motionless. 'Come with me, you've had a dreadful shock.'

She led Rosetta towards the staircase, pulling the door closed to Mr Williams' room. Once they were down on the next floor, Janie guided Rosetta to her own bedroom, easing her down onto the wicker chair beside the dressing table. 'I'm going to leave you here for a few minutes. I need to tell the others what's happened and make a phone call.'

'I don't understand.' Rosetta looked up, her eyes searching Janie's face for confirmation that the last few minutes had been a nightmare, instead of reality. 'Is he really dead? He just arrived this morning.' Rosetta paused, covering her face with her hands. 'Oh no, oh no,' her words were muffled as she sobbed.

'It's a dreadful shock, finding someone like that. I don't know if we should ring the police, but I'm going to ring Dr Filbert, he'll know what to do.' She put her hands on Rosetta's shoulders, but then Rosetta stood, pulling away from her. 'No police,' she said.

'But Mr Williams is a stranger and with him dying suddenly ...I just wondered.'

'What? What did you wonder?' Rosetta's voice was shrill now, her hands gesticulating.

'His next of kin, his family, they will need to be told. Perhaps the police can help.'

'You want my guest house to be a place where people come to die? No police.' Rosetta glared at Janie.

'Don't think about it now, try to close your eyes and rest and as soon as I've phoned the doctor I'll come back to make sure you're alright.'

Having told the others and phoned Dr Filbert, there was little to do but wait, except there was one other person who had been missing from the dining table that evening. Not only had Luigi failed to turn up for supper, but he hadn't even emerged from his room at the sound of Rosetta's scream, or all the comings and goings since.

Janie stepped along the landing and hovered outside Room 2. She tapped lightly on the door. On the second knock she thought she heard a noise from inside the room and decided to gamble. She pushed open the door to find the room was empty. The sash window was open, the curtains flapping against the sill. She walked around the bed to close the window and her foot caught on something. She bent to pick it up and saw that it was a white shirt, crumpled up and stuffed under the bedframe. As she shook the shirt out she noticed a mark on the front, just beside the top button. A mustard coloured lampshade, which hung from the ceiling made the light in the room dim and yellow, but on close examination she had no doubts that the mark was red, blood red. She crumpled the shirt up again and stuffed it back where she'd found it.

Dr Filbert arrived twenty minutes later. Janie showed him to Mr Williams' room and had the strangest feeling she should have knocked before entering. It was difficult to accept that beyond the door lay a dead body and yet just a few hours ago the poor man was probably unpacking his suitcase. Now none of that mattered. Anyone could enter his room, rifle through his personal belongings and he would know nothing of it.

'Shall I leave you to...' Janie said, not knowing what the protocol for such an event might be.

Dr Filbert entered the room and approached the bed, as Janie hovered in the doorway. She couldn't bear to look at the lifeless figure, and yet a small part of her wanted to remember every detail. She watched the GP check the body for a pulse and then saw him shake his head. Mr Williams was laying on top of the bed, partly covered with an orange candlewick bedspread. He was fully dressed, his shirt undone at the collar and his tie slightly loosened.

Feeling increasingly uncomfortable with the idea that she was looking at a dead body, Janie left the doctor to do whatever was necessary and joined the others in the kitchen. Jessica was washing up, stacking the plates and dishes on the work surface. No-one had an appetite. 'I don't know where anything goes and I don't want to go poking around,' she said, as Janie picked up a tea towel. 'Do you think Rosetta will be alright? Should we go and check on her?'

'She's probably trying to sleep, although I bet none of us will have an easy night.' Philip and Greg sat at the kitchen table, ready to spring into action, but struggling to know which action would be most useful. They had all been tossing around unanswered questions and wild theories.

'Poor man,' Philip said. 'If he had a heart condition, it could be the journey was too much for him.'

'It's Rosetta I feel sorry for,' Greg said. 'She had all that worry with Hugh Furness and now this. The poor woman will think she's jinxed.'

'There's no point us second guessing at this stage. It'll be several days before we find out the cause of death. In fact, the police may not even tell us.' Philip spoke his thoughts out loud.

'Why wouldn't they tell us?' Janie said, an edge to her voice.

'Because it's nothing to do with us. We're not family, we're not even friends.'

Greg took Janie's hand in his. 'It must have been horrible, just seeing him, laying there. You must have thought he was asleep at first?'

'Rosetta found him. Then there was that scream. It's ringing in my ears even now.'

'Poor woman,' Philip said, running his fingers through Charlie's fur.

Janie let go of Greg's hand and walked over to the kitchen window. 'I've never seen a dead body before. The dreadful thing was that I found myself fascinated in a strange way. Can I blame it on Poirot, or do you think I'm weird?'

'A man has lost his life,' Greg said, a hint of irritation in his voice. 'How you or I feel about it is pretty irrelevant.'

'It's distressing for you, princess.' Philip stepped in to

defuse the tension. 'But if it was quick, he wouldn't have been in a lot of pain. A sudden ending can be a blessing for the person concerned.'

Janie turned to face her dad. 'There was nothing peaceful about it. His face looked...'

'What? How did he look?' Greg walked over to put his arm around Janie.

'Terrified.'

A quiet cough alerted them that Dr Filbert now hovered in the doorway to the kitchen. 'The body will be removed as soon as the police have been.'

'Was it a heart attack?' Greg asked, looking up at the doctor.

'There will need to be a post mortem, then we'll know for sure.'

Janie led the doctor into the hallway, shook his hand and stepped in front of him to open the front door. 'Thank you for coming so swiftly. It's been a shock for everyone. But Rosetta, that's Mrs Summer, she's taken it very hard.'

'Would you like me to prescribe something? A mild sedative, just to calm her?' Dr Filbert reached into his bag for a prescription pad.

'I'm hoping she'll be alright, I'll take her some strong, sweet tea or on second thoughts, coffee might be better.'

'Try a spot of brandy,' Dr Filbert, lowering his voice to a whisper. 'It won't do her any harm.'

'That must be a first,' Janie smiled, jogged out of her internal thoughts, 'a doctor prescribing alcohol.'

'You didn't hear it from me.' Dr Filbert said, giving Janie a reassuring smile.

Just as the doctor turned to leave, two more visitors appeared on the path leading to the house. One was in police uniform, the other was well known to Janie, Detective Sergeant Frank Bright.

'Mrs Juke,' he said, extending his hand. 'I didn't expect to see you here.'

'DS Bright.' Janie stepped back into the hallway and gestured for the two policemen to enter.

'We understand there's been a death. This is PC Roberts and we've come to inspect the scene.'

'You're talking as though there's been a crime.'

Having heard more voices Greg came through from the kitchen.

'Mr Juke.' DS Bright acknowledged Greg and turned back to Janie. 'We'll see the room now, Mrs Juke.'

'Hadn't you better get Rosetta?' Greg said, putting his hand on Janie's arm. 'We're just visitors, it isn't really our place to show the police around?'

'Rosetta is in no fit state. I'll take them up, I'm sure she won't mind.' Janie turned to the policemen, gesturing for them to follow her through the hallway and up the two flights of stairs to the second-floor guest room where the body of Mr Williams lay.

'You can leave us now. We'll take photos, make notes and inform you when we're done.'

'Photos?'

'Has anyone touched or moved anything in the room since the body was found?'

'No. At least I don't think so.'

'You don't think so?'

'I'm sure Rosetta didn't touch anything. She was in shock. Her scream alerted us, but I'm sure she just froze to the spot. She was still frozen in the same place when I found her, out there on the landing.' Janie's hand moved in the direction of the empty landing, the memory of

Rosetta still sharp in her mind.

'I see, so, just you and Mrs Summer?'

Janie followed the detective's gaze as he surveyed the bedroom. He'd seen something that was making him suspicious. What was it? Before she could ask, he said, 'Close the door on your way out.'

Half an hour later everyone heard the heavy thud of footsteps as DS Bright and PC Roberts descended the staircase. Before anyone spoke, DS Bright gave a little cough. 'I need a few minutes of your time.'

Jessica gestured to the policemen to take a seat, but the detective shook his head. 'We'll be speaking to you individually. Perhaps you could come through to the sitting room, one at a time?'

'I'm sure you understand, we are all visitors here,' Philip said. 'The lady who runs the guest house is a Mrs Summer. She is also the person who found the deceased.'

'Yes, quite. Of course, I will need to interview Mrs Summer, but I'll have a few minutes with each of you first. Is there anyone else I need to speak to?'

'You mean other visitors?' Janie said, sensing the need to be obtuse.

'There's Luigi,' Greg said, ignoring the frown on Jessica's face.

'Luigi?'

'Luigi Denaro. He's another guest,' Jessica volunteered.

'I see. And where is Mr Denaro at this precise moment?'

'I'm not sure,' Janie said.

If DS Bright noticed the exchange of looks between Janie, Greg and Jessica, he chose to ignore them. 'Mr Chandler, will you join us.'

Philip gave a gentle prod to Charlie, who had been dozing. Now he was alert and ready for action, leading Philip through to the sitting room, followed by the detective sergeant and the police constable.

There was little Philip could report about the discovery of the body, other than to confirm he had heard a scream soon after Rosetta left the room to track down her guest.

'And had you already met Mr Williams, prior to this evening?' the detective asked.

'No, he just arrived this morning, as far as I know.'

'I see. Tell me briefly about the people who were present this evening.' The detective sergeant jotted down a few notes as Philip gave him the briefest information about each of the people around Rosetta's table.

'And your daughter followed Mrs Summer upstairs?'

'Not exactly. She went upstairs when we heard the scream.'

'No-one else went with her? Not her husband, for example?'

Philip did not miss the detective's subtle insinuation. 'Janie is very capable,' he said.

'Indeed,' was the detective's terse reply.

Jessica was the next person to be called through to Rosetta's sitting room that had become a makeshift interview room. Like Philip, there was little she could add to the vague picture of events.

'I understand you have just returned from Italy. Is that right Mrs Chandler?'

'It's Miss and yes, I arrived a couple of days ago.'

'And Mr Denaro was your travelling companion?'

'Yes.'

'And was there a particular reason Mr Denaro chose to come to Tamarisk Bay, other than to accompany you?'

'It was a simple coincidence really.'

'I've learned that things are rarely as simple as they might appear.' DS Bright waited, with his pencil hovering over his notebook. The police constable shifted from one foot to the other, as though he was already tiring.

'And do you have any idea where Mr Denaro is right now?' DS Bright removed a packet of cigarettes from his jacket pocket and offered it to Jessica.

'No thanks, I don't smoke.' She wondered if she should fetch him an ashtray and then she realised that he was waiting for her answer to his question. 'I guess he must have gone for a walk.'

DS Bright raised an eyebrow and glanced briefly at the police constable. 'An unusual time to go walking when he was due to join you for supper?'

'Perhaps he went out for a cigarette,' Jessica said, defending her absent friend.

'Ah, yes.' DS Bright made a few more notes and waited for Jessica to continue.

'Has anyone mentioned the missing briefcase to you?'

DS Bright licked the end of his pencil and looked at Jessica.

'Luigi, that's Mr Denaro. Well, his briefcase went missing while we were on the train here from Rome. We reported it to the guard and made a full report when we reached Paris. I'm sure it was a misunderstanding. Someone probably picked it up by mistake. But he was very upset.'

'The guard?'

'No, Luigi.'

'And you think there's a connection between the

missing briefcase and the death of Mr Williams?'

Jessica bit her lip, wishing she hadn't raised the subject. The detective continued to write in his notebook. Jessica tried to see what he had written, but it appeared to be in some kind of shorthand, abbreviated words and squiggles. He paused and looked up. 'And why did Mr Denaro decide to stay here at the *Summer Guest House*?'

'There aren't that many guest houses in Tamarisk Bay. Besides, Janie knows Rosetta. She recommended it to him.'

'Ah, yes, Mrs Juke. She seems to know a lot of people locally.'

'She's the librarian and she's lived in Tamarisk Bay her whole life. She's bound to know everyone.'

'Yes, quite so. And then we have Mr Williams. He also arrived from Italy and made his way to this guest house.'

'Yes.'

'And did you bump into Mr Williams on your train journey here?'

'No.'

'Hm.' DS Bright looked at Jessica, who was now flushed. 'You're sure about that, are you?'

'I'm not sure what you are suggesting, Detective Sergeant.'

'I just ask the questions madam and write down the answers. Well, that's us done for now. Thank you for your time. Constable, take Miss Chandler back to the kitchen and ask Mr Juke to come through.'

While he waited for Greg to join him DS Bright flicked through his notebook. He added a few question marks in one or two places and underlined a couple of statements. Then he looked at his watch. It would be a while yet before he could get home to Nikki and the twins. Not the ideal way to spend Good Friday evening. He guessed his dinner would be waiting for him, on a plate, reading to be warmed up over a saucepan. In truth he should stop off at the police station on his way home to write up his notes more thoroughly, but that could wait until the morning.

Thankfully, an unexpected death in Tamarisk Bay was a rare occurrence, but his instincts told him that this might not be straightforward. Roberts hadn't been on his team for long, but so far had proved useful. Spotting the blood on Mr Williams' pillow showed the constable had a sharp eye. There was a patch of blood to one side of the pillow, which became evident when they moved the body. Then another smaller patch on the underside of the bedspread. But nothing immediately obvious around the victim's face or neck. On DS Bright's instructions Roberts had donned a pair of thin plastic gloves and emptied the waste paper basket that sat in a corner of the room by the window. Underneath two discarded newspapers there was a handkerchief. Roberts shook it out and held it up to his boss. In the centre of the handkerchief was a large patch of blood.

All circumstantial, but evidence nonetheless.

Chapter 7

Good Friday - Summer Guest House

Greg followed the police constable into the sitting room and stood for a moment, not knowing whether the detective sergeant had even noticed him. He seemed to be so engrossed in his notebook. Greg gave a little cough, at which point the detective looked up.

'Mr Juke, take a seat.'

'There's not much I can tell you. I didn't even go upstairs.' Greg wiped his sweating palms down his trousers. All he could think about was why on earth his wife was so attracted to this whole detection lark.

'Let's take it a step at a time. I'm just after a few facts.' DS Bright forced a smile, wondering briefly whether he would have time for a cigarette before the next interview. He held the packet out towards Greg who shook his head. 'Never been a smoker, Mr Juke? I must admit I wish I'd never started, but now I have, well...now what was I saying, ah, yes, had you met Mr Williams before this evening?'

'No.'

'What about Mr Denaro? Have you met him?'

'Not really, no.'

'Be more specific.'

'He arrived with Jessica, that's Janie's aunt. We chatted with him briefly when he was at my father-in-law's house. But then he moved in here.'

'Ah yes. Why was that?'

'What?'

'Why did he move in here?'

'Janie suggested he would be more comfortable here.'

'Ah, your wife.' The detective made another note in his pocketbook and Greg had the dreadful feeling that somehow he had said more than was necessary.

When Janie joined the policemen in the sitting room she couldn't help but reflect on previous conversations with DS Bright. On several occasions she had sat opposite the detective in the police interview room, a barren space that might easily have passed for a prison cell, except for the lack of bars at the door.

'Has anyone offered you a drink?' she said, noticing the expression on the young police constable's face lift at the thought of sustenance.

'A cup of tea would go down very well.' DS Bright replied. 'Roberts can fetch it.' He gestured to the police constable, who withdrew to the kitchen.

'Thirsty work asking questions,' the detective continued. 'But you'll know all about that.'

'My library work usually involved answering questions, pointing people to the right books, that sort of thing.'

'We both know the sort of questions I'm referring to, Mrs Juke. Let's not be coy.'

'How is Nikki? The twins?'

'Let's focus on today's events, shall we?'

'Do you think there is a crime to investigate?'

'I'll ask the questions, Mrs Juke. Tell me exactly what you saw when you walked into Mr Williams' room.'

Janie looked away from the detective, finding it easier to return to the scene in her mind by focusing on a patch of wallpaper behind the detective's head. The paper was yellowed with damp, the edges flicked up, reminding her of the times when, as a child, she loved picking at the wallpaper in her bedroom at home. Then she refocused.

'He was dressed, but he had the bedspread pulled up over him. I assumed Rosetta had covered him up when she found him,' she said.

'We are not in the business of making assumptions, are we?'

She smiled, momentarily grateful for the inclusion. It was as though she had suddenly been promoted from amateur to professional.

DS Bright continued. 'Was his face covered?'

She closed her eyes for a moment, remembering the dreadful expression on the face of Mr Williams. When she opened her eyes again she directed her gaze at the detective. 'No, not his face.'

'Let's start from the moment you met Mr Williams, shall we?'

'We didn't.' Janie fidgeted a little on her chair. 'The only time I saw the poor man was once he'd died.'

'I know you understand the importance of information, Mrs Juke. Every detail can make all the difference.'

'When you're investigating a crime, yes. Do you believe Mr Williams was murdered? Couldn't it be a simple heart attack?' Janie said.

'That's what I'm trying to establish, but all my years in this job have shown me life is rarely plain and simple.

The detective was holding his notebook in such a way it was impossible to see what he was writing. For a moment she wished she had her own notebook with her. At least it would give her something to do with her hands.

'Tell me about your relationship with Mr Denaro.'

'I don't have one. I thought you were here to find out about Mr Williams?'

'When did you first meet Mr Denaro?'

'When he arrived at my dad's house.'

'And your aunt knows him, is that right?'

'He came here with my aunt, from Italy. You already know that, I'm sure. You've spoken to her, haven't you?'

DS Bright sighed. 'Let's have that drink now, shall we?'

PC Roberts had come back into the room with two mugs of tea. A drink was all well and good, but the police constable's thoughts were more about food than drink. It was hours since he'd had his sandwiches and now his thoughts went to the pie and mash his wife had promised him when he'd left home this morning.

'Detective Sergeant, I don't think there is any more I can tell you. Would you like me to fetch Rosetta?' Janie hid a smile as she watched the detective take a sip of his tea, which was clearly not to his liking. 'Did you want sugar? I could fetch some for you, if you like?'

'The tea is just fine.' He took another sip, put the mug down and then turned to Roberts. 'Ask Mrs Summer to join us now, Constable.'

'I'll come up with you. She might be sleeping.' Janie jumped to her feet, ready to follow the police constable.

'Did Dr Filbert prescribe a sedative?'

'No. He did offer, but I'm sure she'll be fine. As long as you don't upset her too much with your questioning.'

For Rosetta Summer having two policemen in her sitting room terrified her almost as much as opening a door and finding one of her guests laying dead.

'Why are you here?' she looked accusingly at DS

Bright. A policeman was drinking from her crockery, sitting on her armchair. Her home would never be the same again.

'Whenever there is a sudden death we need to investigate.' The detective spoke slowly in measured tones, as though Rosetta was a child still learning the language of adults.

'People die. It is not a crime.' Rosetta raised her hands to her face, noticing the chill of her cheeks.

'All we are doing is gathering facts. That's our job, Mrs Summer. Would you like to take a seat while we ask you a few questions?'

'You offer me a seat in my own house?' She made a tutting sound to indicate her irritation, then manoeuvred the other armchair towards the door, sitting as far away from the detective as possible.

'Not too keen on the police?'

'You did nothing to help my husband.'

'Your husband?'

'It was a long time ago. I do not want to speak about it now.'

'As I said, our job is to gather the facts. We are not apportioning any blame...'

Rosetta stood, waving her arms in the air as she spoke. 'Blame? What, you think I bring my guests here then kill them? I want you to leave my house. Go, now.'

'Is everything alright?' Janie pushed open the sitting room door and stepped in to stand beside Rosetta. 'I heard raised voices.'

'Mrs Summer is distressed. Perhaps you could help to reassure her.'

With the situation calmed a little DS Bright attempted to elicit the details of the previous few hours from the perspective of the fractious landlady.

'What can you tell me about Mr Williams?' he asked.

'Tell you? I can tell you nothing. He was a guest in my house, that is all I know.'

'Were you surprised that someone from Italy had booked into your guest house?'

'I am Italian. My friends back home they know what I do. I say to them, come and visit. But no-one comes. They have no money.'

DS Bright watched Rosetta as her hands waved around and her cheeks reddened. He took a cigarette from the packet and put it in his mouth, unlit.

'I would prefer no smoking in my sitting room, please.' Rosetta glared at the detective.

'Of course, quite right.'

'It is an ugly habit. You will smell, your clothes will smell and look at your hands, your fingers, they are yellow. Who wants their fingers to be yellow?' She held out her own hands and studied them, presenting them to the constable as an example of the perfect manicure. The colour on the cheeks of the young police constable changed from pink to red. 'And it is not good for your health,' Rosetta continued. 'Mr Williams, he arrives this morning, he puffs on his pipe, he coughs, then he puffs on his pipe again. And now he is dead.'

DS Bright continued undeterred. 'Did Mr Williams know your friends in Italy?'

'You ask me so many questions, on and on. I don't know Mr Williams. Ask Mr Denaro, he will know more than me.'

'Mr Denaro?'

'They know each other.'

'What makes you think that?'

'Mr Denaro, he speaks to Mr Williams in the morning, when he arrives.'

'I see. And you overheard this conversation?'

Rosetta glanced at the detective sergeant, then looked over at the police constable again. 'You are young, you should be enjoying Easter with your wife. Instead you are here talking about death.'

DS Bright raised an eyebrow, exchanging a brief glance with the constable, whose expression did nothing to suggest if he agreed with Rosetta. In truth, PC Roberts would have agreed with her, if it wasn't for his boss monitoring his every move.

'Let's move on to the events that occurred earlier this evening, shall we?' the detective said, trying to keep a level tone in his voice. 'When you opened the door to the room of Mr Williams, what did you see?'

'You know what I saw. I don't want to say the words aloud. It is like living it again all over.'

'Did you move anything in the room? Did you touch anything at all?'

'No, I did not touch anything. I did not want to go too close.'

'If you didn't touch the body, or even move close to it, how did you know Mr Williams was dead?'

Rosetta's eyes widened. Janie put her arm around her shoulders in a gesture of comfort.

'His eyes, they were open, staring. Santa Maria.' Rosetta made a sign of the cross and bent her head as though in prayer.

'Then one of you must have touched the body, because Mr Williams' eyes were firmly closed when we arrived.'

'I closed them,' Janie said, challenging DS Bright with

a direct glance. 'That's all I did.'

'You didn't touch anything else in the room?' He held his pencil poised over his notebook.

'No. Now, are you finished with us? Mrs Summer needs to rest.'

'We will arrange for the body to be collected later this evening. Please stress on Mr Denaro that I need to speak to him urgently. Ask him to attend the police station at the first opportunity.'

Janie didn't hide her sense of relief as she showed the policemen out.

'I'm sure we'll be speaking again soon, Mrs Juke,' DS Bright said as he shook her hand. 'Meanwhile, please remember this investigation is strictly a matter for the police. You understand what I'm saying?'

'Yes, Detective Sergeant Bright. I understand perfectly.'

She joined the others in the kitchen and made herself a hot drink. For a while, everyone sat in subdued silence, then Greg was the first to speak.

'Love, we really need to go. I promised mum we'd pick Michelle up before ten and by the time we get over there it'll be way past that. Jessica, can we give you and Philip a lift home first?'

'No, it's alright. You two get off. We'll organise a taxi. I just want to speak to Luigi first to make sure he's okay.'

'If you do see him, tell him the police need to speak to him,' Janie said. 'I'll pop up to tell Rosetta we're off.'

Janie padded up to Rosetta's room and pressed her face close to the door. 'Rosetta, it's Janie.'

'Come in.' Rosetta's voice was shaky.

As she stepped into the bedroom Janie noticed the

distinctive smell of perfume that she always associated with her Italian friend. The chintz curtains were drawn and the only light came from a little bedside lamp with a delicate pink shade. To one side of the dressing table was an old pine blanket chest, a wicker chair on the other side. The single bed looked lonely in the centre of the room, with Rosetta looking even lonelier.

'We're heading off soon, but I thought I'd just pop in to say goodbye. Everything's tidied away, you don't need to worry. Are you sure you don't want someone to stay with you? Jessica said she's happy to stay if you'd rather someone was in the house.'

'Mr Denaro is here.'

'Yes, I know, but he's a guest. We thought you might like to have a friend around, just for tonight?'

Rosetta shifted the coverlet back and propped herself up to sitting. Janie noticed she was still dressed. 'No, I will be fine. You must get back to your baby. And your father, he will have been disturbed by all this.'

The case was building in Janie's mind. A dead body, a possible murder, and so far the person she had the most doubts about was a newcomer to Tamarisk Bay, but he was no stranger, he was her aunt's friend. He had behaved oddly over the loss of his briefcase, had skulked around her father's bedroom and there was the bloodied shirt. Rosetta had seen him arguing with Bertrand Williams in the morning and that night poor Bertrand was dead and Luigi nowhere to be found.

She didn't want to alarm Rosetta even more by sharing her fears. But there was something else niggling at her. Something Rosetta had said to DS Bright.

'Rosetta, I just wanted to mention...about Mr Williams...'

'Yes, thank you for saying what you did.'

'It was you who closed his eyes? *Was this what it was like for Poirot, suspecting everyone, even a friend?*'

'Yes.' She covered her face with her hands. 'He reminded me of my husband. That look of shock that life has ended. All hopes and dreams gone. *Pouf.* It was not the face of someone happy to meet our Heavenly Father.'

Janie moved towards the bed, laying her hand on Rosetta's shoulder. 'Why did you not want to tell the police?'

'They mix everything up. You are innocent and they make you feel guilty.'

'You didn't touch or move anything else?'

Rosetta shook her head, her hands still covering her face.

Janie laid her hand on her shoulder. 'I'm sure everything will seem brighter in the morning.'

Chapter 8

Saturday morning - Summer Guest House

A poor night's sleep, with questions tumbling over in her head, meant things appeared far from bright the next morning. Declining her husband's offer to make breakfast, Janie made her way to the guest house.
Hoping to find Rosetta in the kitchen, she tapped lightly on the back door. When there was no reply, she pushed the door a little and called out, 'Rosetta, it's Janie. Are you up and about?' Still receiving no reply, she stepped into the kitchen. An empty coffee cup was on the draining board and a plate with a half-eaten slice of toast on the table. She stayed very still as she listened for any sound or movement. There were noises coming from upstairs, then the sound of someone descending the stairs and a few seconds later Luigi came into the kitchen.

'Good morning,' he said.

'It's hardly a good morning.'

'I've only just got up. Coffee?' He opened two cupboards before finding the cups and saucers. 'There are benefits to staying in a guest house run by an Italian. Real coffee in the morning. Do you think she'll mind if we help ourselves?'

An Italian percolator was sitting on the draining board. Luigi filled it and set it on the gas.

'I didn't see you to say goodbye last night.' Janie said, watching Luigi as he ran his fingers through his hair. 'We were worried about you. And you know the police need to talk to you.'

'I stayed in my room.'

'You weren't in your room when I knocked on the door.'

'I went out for a cigarette.' As though his reply had acted as a reminder he took a cigarette from the packet he was holding and pulled out a miniature lighter from his trouser pocket. 'You don't mind, do you?'

A few months ago, even the lingering smell of cigarette smoke made Janie feel sick, now she just found it mildly distasteful. 'It's fine,' she said, turning away from him slightly so that she didn't need to breathe in the smoke. 'It was a dreadful shock for everyone. But you knew Mr Williams?'

Luigi glared at her. 'Bertie? Yes, I knew him.'

'So you'll know his family? Dr Filbert said we'll need to get in touch with them. There's arrangements to make, a funeral and...'

'I don't know his family.' He puffed on his cigarette until he had finished it and stubbed it out. The coffee bubbled up in the percolator, capturing their attention for a moment.

'Milk?' Janie said, taking a small jug from the fridge.

'It's best drunk strong, hot and black.'

She watched as Luigi poured the coffee. His movements were slow, as though he was still a little sleepy.

'You know the man and he turns up in Tamarisk Bay the day after you. I would say that's more than a coincidence.'

'It's my father's fault.'

Janie waited for him to continue, spooning sugar into her coffee before taking a sip.

'My father knew I was coming here and so he sends his business associate to check up on me.'

'Your dad and Bertie are in business together?'

'No. Bertie runs a property business in and around Anzio. Renting villas out to English tourists.'

'And your father's business?

'My father runs a *successful* business empire, spreading across Italy.'

Janie didn't miss the irony in Luigi's emphasis on the word 'successful'; there was no pride in his voice, the opposite in fact. She was still trying to understand the connection between the two men; she was certain it was relevant.

'Mr Williams isn't related to you, is he?'

'No.'

'Not a kindly godfather looking out for you?' Janie's thoughts flickered to Michelle and she smiled.

'There's nothing kindly about Bertie, or my father.'

'Well, perhaps it's best you telephone your father. Let him know what's happened to his friend. He'll be able to contact Bertie's next of kin. They'll need to decide if he's to be buried here or elsewhere.'

'I have no intention of speaking to my father.'

'Luigi, I don't think you've got any choice.'

'There's always a choice.'

Back home, over a late breakfast, Janie recounted the morning's conversation to Greg. 'It was bizarre. I don't understand any of it and Luigi wasn't exactly forthcoming.' Janie stopped buttering her toast and stood up.

'What's the matter?'

'Did you hear Michelle? I thought I heard her just now. It's almost time for her next feed. I'll go up and fetch her, shall I? I've missed her this morning.'

'You were barely away two hours. She's been as good as gold. The blokes at work don't believe it when I tell them how easy she is. But I reckon we're lucky, mum said she didn't get a decent night's sleep until I was two years old.'

A few moments later, with a sleepy Michelle nestled in her arms, Janie continued. 'All I found out is that Bertie Williams and Luigi's father know each other. And Luigi reckons his father sent Bertie to England to keep an eye on him.'

'It sounds odd. Luigi is hardly a teenager. It would be like Philip sending Jessica to watch out for you. Mind you, now I think about it, I suppose that's not such a bad idea,' Greg teased.

'Seriously though. I pushed him as hard as I could, but he just refused to ring his dad. What else can we do?'

'Maybe Philip can get through to him. Your dad's got a good way with most people. Or Jessica? After all, they're supposed to be friends, aren't they? Perhaps Jessica knows Luigi's father?'

For a few moments Janie was distracted by her daughter, who had started to wriggle. She moved her from one arm to the other and offered Michelle her finger to hold.

'It's so weird, Greg. Luigi turning up, then this Bertie Williams chap dying on his first day here.'

'Oh no, you don't. Don't you dare go putting your Poirot hat on. It's just one of those things. People have heart attacks. Life ends and it doesn't always end as we expect, or where we expect. I'd guess it rarely does. Come on, Michelle, give your dad a cuddle and let your mum finish her toast.'

'I'll walk round to dad's after breakfast and see what he thinks about it all.'

A little later Janie let herself into her dad's house, easing the pram over the door threshold so as not to wake her daughter. But her care was in vain because she hardly had a chance to take her coat off before Michelle started to make grumbling noises.

'Perfect timing,' Janie said, lifting her daughter out of the pram and walking through to the kitchen where Philip was filling the kettle.

Without doubt, in Philip's house, Janie's childhood home, the kitchen was her favourite room. She had so many memories of reading her favourite Poirot stories to her dad, with him testing her to see if she could guess the culprit before they reached the final chapter. They would talk for hours, sitting either side of the kitchen table with Charlie sleeping at their feet.

'Sit yourself down, dad, put your arms out and I'll lay your grand-daughter onto them. She hasn't had enough cuddles from her grandad these last few days. She likes trying to grab your beard.'

'I love the smell of her,' Philip said, holding Michelle close to his face. 'It's a combination of vanilla and something else, lavender maybe, or violets?'

'Not when her nappy needs changing, it isn't.' Michelle stretched one arm out, trying to grab Philip's face. 'Hey, you be careful with grandad's beard. I need to cut her fingernails. They may be tiny, but they still scratch when she grabs you.'

'Your mum used to bite yours, rather than use scissors.'

Janie wasn't sure she wanted the images that came into

her mind at the mention of her mum. 'Anyway, where's Jessica?' she said.

'She's gone for a walk. Says she needs to clear her head.'

'Not the homecoming she was expecting, that's for sure. How much has she told you about Luigi?'

'Reading between the lines I think she's wishing she never agreed to him joining her.'

'Why?'

'With all that fuss he made over his briefcase going missing, she's seen another side to him that's made her uncomfortable.'

'She thinks he's dodgy?'

'All we have at the moment is supposition and guesswork, so don't go getting ahead of yourself, thinking this is a case that needs solving.'

'You and Greg make a good double act, he's just told me the same thing. Here's more for you to think about. Rosetta was right, Luigi does knows Bertie.'

'Bertie?'

'Bertie Williams. The man who died last night. Luigi's father and Bertie know each other.' She closed her eyes while she mulled over her thoughts. 'Dad, there's more to all of this, I'm certain. I didn't worry you, but that first night when Luigi stayed here...' She hesitated, replaying her thoughts.

'You didn't just suggest he moved out because he was being squashed in the box room, did you?'

Janie smiled. 'I don't know why I ever think I can keep secrets from you.'

Philip patted the chair for his daughter to sit beside him. 'And you want to know what to do and who to tell?' he said, after Janie explained her doubts and fears about her aunt's friend.

'Am I seeing things that aren't there? It's one thing to catch someone poking around in your bedroom, quite another to start accusing them of murder.'

'You've got no choice, love. You must go to the police. Tell them everything you know and let them sort it out. Meanwhile you can't leave him staying with Rosetta. We'd never forgive ourselves if something else happened. Do you want me to speak to him?'

'That was Greg's suggestion. He said you've got a good way with you. He might have been suggesting that I haven't.'

Philip smiled. 'Let's just say you can be a little pushy at times, over-enthusiastic.'

Janie stretched over and lifted her daughter from Philip's arms. 'Come on, Michelle, we know when we're being reprimanded. Ha, look at that, she doesn't want to let go of you,' Janie said, prising her daughter's hands away from Philip's face.

'Although it's your enthusiasm that makes you so special. Indomitable, I'd say.' Philip smiled. 'But this time I think you might be adding two and two together and making five or six.'

'I hope you're right, dad. Poor Jessica, if it turns out that Luigi is a really bad lot, well, she'll be desperate. She'll think it's her fault, bringing him here to Tamarisk Bay, to our home.'

Janie took a deep breath, before continuing. 'Dad, there's something else. Don't be angry with me, but you don't think Jessica knows more than she's saying about Luigi?'

'I'm not even going to answer that. You're forgetting everything you know about your aunt. You're forgetting the most important thing that all good investigators rely on. Your instincts. You need to trust them, princess. We need to find out as much as we can about Luigi, so we can base our understanding on the facts. All your Poirot training should have taught you that.'

'You sound like DS Bright,' Janie said, sighing.

'Hopefully not.'

Chapter 9

Saturday morning - Tidehaven Police Station

Frank Bright stifled a yawn as he turned away from the desk sergeant. The last few weeks had been difficult for his wife Nikki, as she tried to bear the brunt of the responsibility for the twins. Two months on and there was still no chance of establishing a daily routine. Luke had developed a feeding problem and it was increasingly difficult to settle him. As the boys were still sharing a cot, when Luke woke, so did Tom. It was a relentless cycle. As much as his wife reassured him she was managing, the dark circles around her eyes told him a different story.

He looked at the telephone, lifted the receiver and replaced it again. Each morning he rang his wife to check all was well, but this morning he needed to prepare his interview questions for Luigi Denaro. The desk sergeant had informed him Mr Denaro had presented himself at the front desk a little after 9am. He had been put in the interview room and asked to wait. Twenty minutes had passed and he guessed the Italian would be getting agitated. Agitated could be useful, it meant emotions were not so carefully controlled. And once control was lost, the truth often emerged. At least that had been Frank's experience in many of the criminal cases he had dealt with. But this case was an odd one.

Strangers come into town and then there is an unexplained death. Of course, it could have been natural causes, but until the post-mortem results came through he wasn't taking any chances.

He lit a cigarette, savouring the momentary lift it gave him. Since the twins were born Nikki had asked him not to smoke in the house. She'd got it into her head it could harm the babies. Something about an article she'd read, or some doctor's warning on TV. He didn't mind pandering to her request, she didn't ask for much, but his professional life was founded on the idea that nothing was proved until there was concrete evidence. Maybe there was enough research out there to prove the link, but until he'd read it for himself he wasn't going to change his mind.

He took another quick look through the list of questions he'd jotted down, finished his cigarette and walked through to the interview room. Glancing through the pane of glass in the door, he watched Luigi Denaro pacing across the room. As soon as Frank pushed open the door Luigi stopped and turned to face him.

'You have kept me waiting a long time.'

'Good morning. I'm Detective Sergeant Frank Bright.'

'I didn't plan to spend the whole morning here at the police station.'

'You're a busy man, sir?'

Luigi looked at the detective, trying to work out whether his remark was genuine or sarcastic.

'Thank you for coming in.' Frank continued.

'Janie told me you asked to see me. I don't know why,' Luigi said.

'Janie? As, yes, Mrs Juke.'

Frank couldn't decide if the involvement of Janie Juke in this case was likely to be a help or a hindrance. At times she was like a splinter he couldn't extricate, but he had to admit that on occasion she had also proved useful.

'You are currently staying at the *Summer Guest House,* is that correct?'

'Yes.'

'How did you come to stay at this particular guest house?'

'I needed a room, there was a vacancy. I don't understand why you are asking me such things.'

'What is your relationship with Mrs Summer?'

Luigi frowned and waited.

'The landlady of the guest house where you are currently residing,' Frank continued.

'I don't have a relationship with Mrs Summer. I am a paying guest, that is all.'

'But you are both Italian?'

'There are many Italians here in England, but they are not all related to each other. Anyway, I am also half-English.' Luigi didn't try to disguise his irritation.

'Let's move on to yesterday's events. You had been invited to join Mrs Summer and her friends for a dinner party.'

'Yes.'

'What time did you join them?'

'I don't know what you mean.'

'Mr Denaro, I realise English may not be your first language, but you appear to have a fluent command of it. So I'm struggling to see what you don't understand about the question. It's very straightforward. What time did you join everyone at the table for supper?'

'I didn't.'

'You didn't?'

'No.'

'And why was that?'

'I was in my room, resting.'

'Resting?'

'Yes, I had a headache.'

'Ah, I see.'

Frank took the cigarette packet from his jacket pocket and offered it to Luigi, who took a cigarette, lit it and took a long drag.

'So, to recap,' DS Bright continued, 'you had been invited to join the others for supper, but you declined because you had a headache?'

'No. I was going to join them, but then there was the incident.'

'And what incident would that be?'

'You know well enough what incident. It's the reason you've asked me here, isn't it?'

'Are you referring to the death of Mr Williams?'

'Yes.'

Luigi wiped the sweat from his forehead and then placed his hands on the table in front of him. 'I haven't done anything wrong.'

'Mr Denaro, let me make myself clear. I have asked you here today to ascertain the facts. I'm not sure how the law works in Italy, but here in England you need to understand I could arrest you for withholding information.'

'I'm not withholding anything.'

Frank watched a bead of sweat run down Luigi's forehead, but this time the Italian didn't move to wipe it away. Instead his hands remained on the table, but his fists were now clenched.

'Tell me about your relationship with Mr Williams.'

'What has Janie said?'

'Mrs Juke has said nothing. Why, what is it she knows?' Frank tapped his pencil on the table so forcefully

82

the lead broke. He stood and walked to the plastic
rubbish bin in the corner of the room and dropped the
pencil into it. Then he returned to the table, took
another pencil from his jacket pocket and sat again.

'Mr Williams knows my father. Or rather he knew my
father.'

'I see. So, Mr Williams is a family friend?'

'No, I didn't say that. He knows my father. It's a
business relationship, that's all.'

'Did you know Mr Williams was coming to Tamarisk
Bay?'

'No.'

'So, you were surprised to see him?'

'Yes.'

'And what conversation did the two of you have on
the day he died?'

'None.'

'I find that hard to believe. Here is a man who you
have met through his association with your father. He
turns up in Tamarisk Bay, days after your own arrival, and
you didn't speak to him? I'll remind you again, Mr
Denaro, that lying to a police officer is a serious offence.'

Luigi stood, pushing the chair away so roughly it fell
to the floor.

'You have a temper, Mr Denaro,' the detective said.

'Is this the way you treat all your visitors to this town?'
Luigi picked up the chair and pushed it towards the table.
'Am I a suspect? Has there been a crime? If not, then I
would like to leave now. I have given you enough of my
time.'

'Of course, you are free to leave. Just one question
before you go.'

Luigi walked towards the door, pausing with his hand

on the handle, but with his back towards the detective.

'I understand that during your journey here from Italy an item of luggage went missing.'

'Yes, my briefcase, it was stolen.' Luigi turned to face Frank Bright. 'Do you have news of it? Has it been found?'

'Describe the briefcase to me.'

'Italian leather, two pockets in the front, a handle. It was a briefcase, I don't know how much more I can tell you.

'We will let you know if it turns up. In the meantime, I'd like you to remain in Tamarisk Bay. We may need to question you again.'

Frank Bright spoke to the desk sergeant on the way back to his office. 'Where's Roberts?'

'Out in the patrol car, sir.'

'Tell him I need to see him as soon as he's back. It looks as though we need to make another visit to the *Summer Guest House.*'

Chapter 10

Saturday afternoon - Summer Guest House

The welcome Janie received from Rosetta a little later that day was curt. Returning to the guest house, Janie rang the front doorbell, then rattled the knocker.

'Yes, yes, I'm coming.' Rosetta's distinctive accent was unmistakeable and as the door opened it revealed the landlady with her face flushed and tense.

'Janie. What do you want?'

'I don't want anything. I just popped by to see if you were alright.' She lifted Michelle from her pram and passed her to Rosetta. 'I thought a cuddle might help, you've had a difficult twenty-four hours. And this is Barnaby, her favourite bear. She likes to chew his ears.'

Rosetta ran her fingers over Michelle's face and was rewarded with a little gurgle. 'So soft, your baby's skin is so perfect.'

'I was here this morning, but you must have still been in your room. I was worried about you.'

They walked through to the kitchen where Rosetta stood looking out of the window, her face turned away from Janie.

'A difficult twenty-four hours. Yes, you are right.'

For a while the only noise to be heard was a gentle cooing sound from Michelle, reminding Janie of a collared dove she insisted on rescuing when she was little. The baby dove had fallen out of its nest and Janie persuaded her dad and Jessica to let her rear it until it was strong enough to fly off. The day it left she sat at the window all day, hoping it might return.

'It would be nice to be a baby again,' Rosetta said, moving away from the window and bending to kiss the baby's forehead. 'They have food and love, they want nothing else.'

'I know what you mean. Being a grown up isn't much fun sometimes. But at least we get to make choices.'

'You make decisions for Michelle now, but when she is older she will decide for herself and you will have to stand by and watch her make bad choices sometimes.' Rosetta bowed her head and turned away from Janie.

'What happened to Mr Williams is very sad, more than that, it's been a dreadful shock. But there's something else troubling you, isn't there? Do you want to talk about it?'

'I left my mother, my whole family, to come to England.'

Janie moved to put her hand on Rosetta's arm.

'But you fell in love, you followed your husband here.'

'And then he dies and I am here, alone.' Rosetta wiped her hands down her dress, as if she was trying to wipe away the melancholy weighing her down. 'Take no notice of me. I am okay. I will sing to your baby, a song my mother always sang to me.'

'Shall I leave you for a bit while I pop upstairs to see if Luigi is in?' When she was pregnant Michelle's movements inside her were a welcome sensation, but the fluttering in her stomach now was far from welcome. Nevertheless, she kept her voice light. 'I'm trying to persuade him to ring his father. Someone needs to pass on the sad news to the family of Mr Williams.'

Once upstairs she tapped on Luigi's door. 'It's me, Janie. Can I come in?' Hearing a grunt from inside the room she eased the door open, to find Luigi laying on his bed, with his feet hanging over the end of the bed and his head resting on his hands.

'Are you okay to chat? Just for a few minutes? I've left Michelle with Rosetta, but she'll be wanting a feed any minute.' She walked further into the room, waiting for him to acknowledge her. 'I'll sit here, if that's okay?' she said, pulling a chair over from the window. 'Don't forget the police want to speak to you.'

'I have seen them, this morning.'

'I'm pretty sure they are just going through the motions, but what with Mr Williams dying suddenly and you knowing him...'

'Did you tell the police that I know him?'

'Rosetta might have mentioned it. It's not a secret, though, is it? I'm guessing you'll want to help the police if you can.' She studied his face. Was this the face of a murderer? Hadn't Poirot taught her not to ignore the obvious. Weren't most murderers known to their victims?

'Help them with what? Bertie had a heart attack. I don't understand why the police are involved.'

Janie shifted on her chair, looking out of the window, mentally rehearsing her words before she spoke. 'The thing is, Luigi, you know I came to look for you on the night Bertie died.' She continued, without waiting for his response. 'I went into your room and found something.'

'You had no business poking around in my things.'

'I didn't poke around. I was looking for you, instead I found something I wish I hadn't seen.'

Luigi's face was without expression. He barely blinked and for a moment Janie was reminded of a waxwork model she'd seen in Madame Tussaud's on a school trip, lifeless, without emotion.

'Don't interfere in things you know nothing about,' he said.

'Tell me then and I'll push the incident from my mind. I found a shirt of yours, with blood on it.'

'I cut myself shaving.'

'The shirt was stuffed under the bed, as though someone was trying to hide it.'

'I have nothing to hide. If the shirt was under the bed I must have dropped it.'

On each of the cases she had worked on Janie found that events in the past held clues to mysteries in the present. A visit to the site of Joel's death had helped during her search for Zara. Then, when she worked for Hugh Furness, everything she needed to know to solve the case came from delving into events that had taken place years before. Perhaps the same approach would work now, whether or not this turned out to be a case that needing solving.

'Have you had any more news about your missing briefcase?'

'Stolen briefcase.' He made no attempt to disguise the anger in his voice. 'Nothing yet. I know you like to investigate mysteries, but you can forget about this one. There are no mysteries here.'

Downstairs, Rosetta tutted when the front door bell rang. She opened the door to find PC Roberts standing on the doorstep.

'There is no more to tell you, please go away.' Rosetta went to close the door, but the policeman held it open with his boot.

'You'll have to let me in, Mrs Summer. There's something I need to collect from Mr Winters' room.'

'What something? Tell me and I will fetch it.'

'I'm sorry, madam, but this is a police investigation. It's important you let the police go about their business as they see fit.'

'You need a warrant. To search. I know, I have seen it on the television. Come back with a warrant.'

'Mrs Summer, I'm not doing a search of your house. I'm here to pick up something we saw when we were here yesterday.'

Rosetta sighed, stood back and watched the policeman step past her.

'You know the room. I am not coming with you. Take what you want and then please leave.'

PC Roberts made his way to Room 3, carried out his boss's instructions and returned to the hallway to find Rosetta still standing by the front door ready to show him out. In his hands he held a leather briefcase.

'Mr Denaro's briefcase, you have found it,' she said, holding her hands as if to take it from him. 'Wait. He is here with Janie. I will fetch him, he will be so happy.'

PC Roberts held his hand up, hoping to stop Rosetta from moving. 'No, madam. But please ask Mr Denaro to come to the police station this afternoon. We would like to question him further.'

'You with your questions,' she said, shaking her fist at the back of the policeman as he departed.

Ensuring Michelle was content and occupied with her favourite Barnaby bear, Rosetta went up to Room 2 to give Luigi the news about his briefcase. She expected at least a smile. Instead, he pushed her aside without a word. They followed him along the corridor until they all stood outside Room 3.

'Luigi, you mustn't go in there. You'll be disturbing the scene and it will get you into more trouble.'

Ignoring Janie's advice, Luigi pushed open the door. Rosetta and Janie stood on the landing watching him as he slid open each drawer of the tallboy, rifling through them, with little apparent concern for the mess he was leaving behind. Then he walked over to the wardrobe.

'I really don't think you should be doing this,' Janie said, feeling more anxious by the minute.

'I understand nothing.' Rosetta put her hand on Janie's shoulder. 'Why is he looking? The police have his briefcase. Why is he not happy?'

'He wants to know why it was in Bertie's room,' Janie whispered, feeling like a co-conspirator.

They watched as Luigi pulled out two suits on hangers and threw them onto the bed. He put his hand into each of the trouser pockets and pulled out a couple of bus tickets, which he threw onto the floor. Continuing his search, he dipped his hand into an outside pocket of the jacket and pulled out more tickets, not bus tickets this time. The tickets were folded, so he opened them out, flattening them with his hand.

'There, I knew it.' He thrust the tickets at Janie, who looked at them and waited for an explanation.

'He was on our train. I knew it was him, I didn't imagine it. I saw him and he saw me. And then he stole my briefcase.'

The two women looked at each other and then Rosetta shrugged her shoulders. 'I understand nothing. I am going downstairs to your baby, she is crying for her milk.'

The first cries from Michelle hadn't escaped Janie's ears, but she knew there was still at least half an hour before her daughter was due her next feed.

'I'll be down in a minute,' she called out to Rosetta, who was already half-way down the stairs. Then, turning to Luigi, she said, 'Think about it, Luigi. There's no reason why Bertie would steal your briefcase. It doesn't make any sense. How would he even have known which compartment you were in?'

Without replying, Luigi brushed past Janie.

'If you're going to the police station, I'll come with you,' she said, following him downstairs. But by the time she had settled Michelle into her pram, she heard the front door close. Luigi had left.

Frank Bright asked PC Roberts to show Luigi through to the interview room.

'You have my briefcase,' Luigi said, as soon as the detective walked in. 'I would like it back.'

'All in good time. First of all, I'd like to know why Mr Williams had your briefcase.'

'You want me to know the mind of a dead man? But I do know he was on the same train as me, the train where my briefcase was stolen.'

'What makes you think that?'

'I thought I had seen him on the train and now I have proof.' Luigi took the train tickets from his jacket pocket and slid them across the table towards the detective.

'Where did you get these?' the detective asked.

'From Bertie's jacket.'

'You are treading on very thin ice, Mr Denaro. You are giving me more than one reason to make you my number one suspect.'

'For a suspect, you need a crime.'

'We'll see about that. Are you sure there's nothing else

you want to tell me about the night Mr Williams died?'

The stand-off between the two men continued, each trying to outstare the other.

'I have nothing more to tell you.'

'I'd like your passport, Mr Denaro.'

'I'm not planning on going anywhere.'

'In that case you won't be needing it.' Frank held his hand out and waited a few moments before Luigi slowly put his hand inside his jacket and pulled out his passport.

'There,' he said, slapping it into the detective's hand.

'We may need to speak to you again, but for now you are free to go.'

'My briefcase, please.' Luigi held the detective's eye gaze; it was as though they were two children challenging each other to a playground fight.

PC Roberts had been standing silently behind Frank Bright. Now the detective nodded to him and the policeman left the interview room. A few moments later he returned with a large plastic bag.

Luigi stood, holding his hands out to receive his belongings. PC Roberts removed the briefcase and put it on the table in front of the detective.

'Your briefcase, Mr Denaro.' Frank said, watching Luigi's reaction.

Luigi's response was evident in his body language. He dropped his hands down to his side and his shoulders slumped forward. 'It's not mine,' he said. It was as though he had lost it all over again.

Chapter 11

Easter Sunday - Tamarisk Bay

The peace of St Augustine's church was better than any treat for Rosetta. Sited just at the back of Tensing Gardens, the nineteenth century church was surrounded by a well-tended graveyard. The footpath leading to the front of the church was edged with rhododendrons and azaleas, which were yet to flower.

Often, when Rosetta had a free afternoon, she would visit and sit quietly in one of the pews. There was nothing oppressive about the silence. Instead, it was as though she could empty herself into it. She liked to run her hand along the old oak pews, which were soft and worn. Before each religious festival volunteers offered up their time to rub beeswax into the timbers, filling the church with the scent of honey and incense.

On Rosetta's regular visits, after a few moments of prayer, she would walk around the church, gaze at each of the Stations of the Cross and wonder how a man, albeit a holy man, had been able to take on so much pain. When she reached the little oak table beside the front door, she would light candles, one each for her mother and father and one for her husband.

Today she would have to share the church with a busy Easter Sunday congregation, many who never set foot in the church week after week. Given the chance to parade proudly in front of their neighbours they would suddenly remember their Catholic faith and arrive in their best coat and hat.

She reached the church later than usual, dipping her

hand into the holy water by the entrance and making a sign of the cross, then bringing her fingers to her lips. It was a ritual she had repeated since she was little, copying everything her mother did, fascinated by the mystery of the Holy Trinity; the Father, the Son and the Holy Ghost, three spirits in one.

She was pleased to find space in one of the pews at the back. She caught the gaze of a couple of women she recognised from the Catholic mothers' meeting group. She had attended it just twice, but as she wasn't a mother and she was the only Italian, she felt out of place, despite the welcome they gave her.

The organ music sounded and she stood, ready to sing the first hymn. It was strange to sing the words in English, even after all these years. Since she left her home town in Puglia, not a day passed when the family and friends she had left behind weren't in her thoughts. She had met her husband towards the end of the war, married him soon after and then thought nothing of following him back to England. It was five years before they were able to save the money for a visit home and in that time her father had passed away.

Jack had been a good husband. He was lucky to get work after the war. So many soldiers returning and more still never to return. He worked long hours in a factory. She hated the smell he brought home with him each evening, chemicals that seeped into his clothes, his skin. She was certain the place contributed to his illness and subsequent death, although the authorities had disagreed with her. *There is no link* they told her. But whenever she thought about it, which was often, she wanted to scream and shout. Someone should be punished, someone was to blame.

The mass was proceeding now and she watched as the children walked up to the altar to take Holy Communion. It was a tradition in this church that the children lined up first, then the elderly, who were slow to move, often leaning on the arm of a son or daughter. The rest of the congregation followed, the whole process taking as much as twenty minutes when the church was full. There was time for prayer and quiet reflection, until it was her turn to walk to the altar and receive the host.

Today she had more to pray for than usual. There were so many conflicting thoughts and concerns running through her mind that she was grateful for a chance to close her eyes, to empty her mind, just for a while. For the last two nights it had been impossible to sleep. In the early hours of Sunday morning she had made her way downstairs to sit for a while by the kitchen window, staring out at the black night.

The death of a guest and then the police arriving at her door had filled her with dread. By the time they had finished questioning her it was as though she had been through a mangle, her emotions stretched and flattened. They had prodded and poked around the bedroom, taking photographs. The whole thing made her feel violated, like her home was tainted by dirty secrets.

The mass had ended. People were filing past her. She moved to one side in the pew to allow a couple to slide out. She had half an hour or so before she needed to catch the bus to Tidehaven, to visit her in-laws. In a few minutes she would have the church to herself again.

When everyone had left she moved over to the little oak table. She picked at the wax that had pooled around the bottom of the candles, then she took the taper. Once it was lit she lifted candles from the metal box that sat on a nearby chair, dropping a few coins into the nearby dish. As she lit each candle she said a silent prayer. One, two, three... she hesitated, then she lifted a fourth candle from the box. And as this last candle flickered into life, she said a fervent prayer that all would be well.

The Easter tradition in the Chandler household was for a cooked breakfast, followed by swapping of Easter eggs. For the last couple of years Greg had been happy to spend Easter Sunday morning at Philip's house, where a lazy breakfast would be followed by a Sunday roast. Janie returned the favour, visiting her in-laws, Nell and Jimmy Juke, for afternoon tea. This year, with everyone wanting to fuss over the baby, the plan was to follow the same schedule.

By the time Janie and Greg arrived at Philip's, Jessica had already laid out a tempting breakfast spread. The aroma and sounds of sizzling bacon greeted them as they arrived. Michelle was passed around like a little pink parcel, until it was time for her feed. Then Jessica sat with her nestled in her arms, while Janie took over in the kitchen.

'This takes me back, I remember an Easter Sunday morning when you were just a baby,' Jessica said, smiling at Janie.

'How old would you have been?'

'Oh, I was an awkward teenager, but your mum was more than happy to hand you over. Particularly when it was nappy changing time.' Jessica winked, before noticing Philip's expression change. 'Sorry, Phil, that was thoughtless of me.'

'No, it's fine.'

'Mum made her choices a long time ago. It was just a

shame they didn't include us, eh, dad?' Janie put her hand on Philip's shoulder and gave it a squeeze. 'And now she's missing out on her first grandchild.'

'Let's change the subject, shall we?' Greg interrupted.

'Yes, food is beckoning,' Philip and Charlie made their way through to the dining room. 'You've laid a place for Luigi?'

'He had an open invitation. I thought he'd be here by now.' There was a note of irritation in Jessica's voice. 'Perhaps he's gone to mass with Rosetta?'

'Let's not wait, there's plenty for him when or if he turns up,' Philip said.

Once breakfast was over and Jessica had gone upstairs to retrieve some Easter gifts, the doorbell rang.

'You're just in time for chocolate, but too late for anything remotely savoury,' Janie quipped when Luigi came through to the dining room.

'I was held up.' His face was dark with what may have been tiredness, or could have been something else. Each time Janie studied his expression she tried to imagine what would make one man take the life of another. Would such a traumatic event be forever etched on the criminal's face, would it be there behind his eyes, in his sideways glances? She shook her head to chase the sombre thoughts away.

'Let's leave the clearing up to dad and Jessica. You and I can take Michelle for a stroll. It's about time I showed you a few of the Tamarisk Bay highlights,' Janie said. 'Let's go and explore *Bottle Alley*. Come to think of it, Michelle hasn't seen it yet either. Grab your jacket then and give us a hand with the pram.'

She was taking her precious baby daughter out for a

walk with a man who might have darkness in his heart. But her dad had said to trust her instincts. Right now those instincts were telling her that Luigi had secrets to hide, but those secrets were not about murder.

Luigi followed Janie and once they were out on the street, they walked side by side in silence for a while. When they reached the seafront, Janie pointed towards the underpass. 'That's where we're headed. The alleyway dates back to the thirties, I think. You need to use your imagination to picture it as it was when they first created it. Originally, there were windows all down this side to protect people from the sea spray, but look at the walls, they're covered in millions of pieces of coloured glass. Clever, eh?'

Luigi gave a cursory glance towards the concrete walls, studded with fragments of every colour. Even though the underpass ran alongside the beach, the air had a stagnant quality, as if the smells of seaweed and dead fish arrived on the wind and never managed to quite leave. They reached an empty stone seat and Janie sat, pointing to the space beside her. 'Let's stop for a while.'

Luigi sat beside her, kicking at some rubbish on the ground below the seat. Then he took his cigarettes out and lit one. 'The police have taken my passport.'

'Did they say why?'

'They think I'm guilty of something. You think I am too, don't you?' He looked up now, staring into Janie's face in a way that made her feel uncomfortable.

'I wasn't trying to accuse you yesterday,' she said. 'I'm just trying to understand.'

'It's not an easy story to explain.'

'I know fathers and sons don't always get on. I'm lucky with my dad, he's so easy going.'

Janie had positioned the pram on her right-hand side. Without the movement of being pushed along, Michelle started to wriggle and complain. Janie picked up Barnaby bear from the foot of the pram and tucked him in beside her daughter, who immediately tried to grab his ear and bring it to her mouth to chew.

'If you don't want to speak to your dad, how about you phone your mother? Perhaps she would act as intermediary? Someone needs to contact Mr Williams' family.'

Janie waited for him to respond. She watched as he tightened his hands into fists, as though he was trying to draw strength to speak.

'My mother is dead,' he said. His words were like blocks of lead bearing down on him.

'I'm so sorry, Luigi.' Janie said. Anything she could think of to say now seemed facile, any questions irreverent. She rocked the pram to and fro, giving herself time and space to absorb his words.

He finished his cigarette, then he jumped up, his sudden movement making her turn around. He moved over to the far side of the underpass, turning away from her to face the sea. She sensed her next question may remain unanswered, that if she said the wrong thing he would close up and offer nothing more.

'Were you very young when she died?'

'My mother lived with great sadness, the whole of her life.'

'Depression can be a terrible thing.'

'Depression suggests an illness. My mother was not ill. She was sad. Life had treated her badly.'

He remained standing with his back towards her. They both listened to the crash of the waves as they tumbled onto the shingle.

'It must be so difficult for your father, he must miss her dreadfully.'

'My father is not a nice man.'

'He's not violent, is he?'

For a moment Luigi considered her question. At least a violent rage would have shown emotion, instead of the cold absence that tainted all the memories of his childhood, his adolescence. 'Nothing like that. My mother was not a strong person. I don't mean her health, that was robust enough, but her character was fragile. She needed someone to lean on. She thought my father was that someone, he is strong in every sense of the word. No-one messes with Alberto Denaro.' Luigi's voice became increasingly hushed as he spoke of his parents. Each time he paused, the only background sound they heard was the swish of the pebbles and the occasional seagull.

'It was a marriage of contrasts, two people who were looking for different things. He wanted a wife to bear him a son, and once I was born she'd done her job.'

'I'm sure they loved each other.'

'Perhaps,' he said, shaking his head. 'But I never once saw them laugh together, or hold hands.'

They remained silent for a while, each in their own thoughts, until the sound of Michelle's cries brought Janie back to the present. She had thrown the bear aside and was now missing him.

'My mother's name was Eloise.'

'That's a pretty name.'

'Yes, and she was pretty too. But I would often come home from school and find her in tears, for no apparent reason. I started to spot the signs. Some days she would barely speak, she chose to close herself off from the world.'

'And your father?'

'He was always so busy. I don't think he even noticed.'

'Is that why you are so angry with your father?'

He turned to face Janie and lit another cigarette. 'Let's walk for a while.'

They walked slowly along the underpass. A couple of lads cycled past them racing each other and laughing.

After a few minutes, Luigi pointed to another seat and they both sat again.

'Your dad is a very special man.' Luigi's voice was heavy with emotion. 'You are lucky.'

Janie waited, sensing he was going to say something else and then he said, 'Your mother left when you were young?'

Janie closed her eyes tight.

'You don't want to talk about it, I understand that.'

'I was little. I didn't understand everything that went on. All I know is that she walked out on us when dad needed her the most.'

'And you? What did you need?'

She dropped her hands and looked at him. There was a challenge in his gaze.

'We had Jessica.'

'A surrogate mother?'

'More like a big sister. She brought light to what could have been a dark time.'

'You were lucky.'

He finished his cigarette and threw it on the ground, stubbing it out underneath his shoe. 'Before she died my mother told me a story, about an English soldier she met in Anzio, during the war.'

'Not your father?'

'No.'

'Can you bear to tell me that story, Luigi?'

He brushed his hair back from his face, turned to face the sea and then began to speak.

Chapter 12

1944 - the piazza

There was to be a wedding. Love blossoming in the midst of conflict and death. Soon, two people would emerge from the church of Santa Teresa, with their witnesses, but without the usual floral tributes, the daintily dressed entourage. None of these were possible. At least she guessed as much. It would be nothing more than two people declaring their love for each other.

She perched on a wall outside the bar on the corner of Via Cesare and Via Lombardi. As she looked to her left she could see the sea. In the distance, the water appeared as still as glass. Yet close to her, in the harbour, the turbulence reflected all she had experienced since the outbreak of war. Fishing boats bumped against the harbour wall, bruising what was left of their paintwork. Much of it had flaked away, burnt off by a combination of hot summer sun and fierce autumn gales.

When her family first moved to Italy she knew nothing of its seasons. Now she knew that the sun shone most days, but when it was accompanied by the swirling air coming straight off the Mediterranean, then it was easier to close her eyes and remember home.

Just months ago the Anzio beaches were the site of bloodshed, thousands of men killed or injured. Torpedoes, bombing, tanks, noise and terror. She had hidden indoors for weeks, afraid to step outside, for fear of what she might see. But today she would take a risk. The sun was shining and it was time.

Bar Centrale was her favourite of all the little Italian

cafés, but since the outbreak of war it had been closed. This wasn't a time for pleasure, instead the streets were filled with soldiers, armoured vehicles and desolation. Before Luigi was born she would come and sit at one of the little café tables and enjoy everything about the dark liquid in the miniature cup. The first time she was served an espresso she felt as if she had landed in Alice's storybook world. A tea party where the handle on the cup was so small she could barely fit a finger inside it to lift it to her lips. The hot, strong liquid became her drink of choice. She loved the slight bitterness that remained after she stirred the sugar, until she could no longer feel the grains grinding at the bottom of the cup. The Italians often drank this little shot of caffeine in one go, but she liked to sip it, savouring the aroma each time she lifted the cup to her lips. But it was so long since she had tasted real coffee. The treacle-like liquid made of chicory was a poor substitute.

All the food she had come to love had been replaced by whatever could be scavenged. Even bread was scarce, once the heart and soul of the Italian meal, the traditional *paniotta* was almost impossible to find. Instead people made bread from potato flour. Families outside the town, with land enough to grow vegetables, were the lucky ones.

From her seat on the low wall she had a clear view of the piazza, but instead of looking at the pavements covered with rubble from the latest bombings, she closed her eyes. She remembered her last visit to the piazza before war was declared. Two small boys were sitting on the edge of the marble fountain, dipping their hands in the water and splashing each other, gleeful expressions on their faces. Two women sat side by side on a nearby bench, engrossed in their conversation. Occasionally one of the women would throw her hands in the air. When she first arrived in Italy she hadn't understood these gesticulations. Every discussion appeared to be an argument, voices raised, expressions lively. Then, over time, she learned the topic might be as simple as the rising price of peaches, or the joy that followed a bumper harvest. Food was at the heart of life for the Italian people, the focus for their every day.

In her first few years here the everyday was taken up with schoolwork. The family had moved to Anzio when she was fifteen and for a long time she stumbled over the language. Her father showed his displeasure by shunning her each time she made a grammatical error. The fear of getting it wrong made it worse. Often she knew the words, but they remained hidden somewhere inside her head, scared to emerge onto her tongue. Even when she spoke in English her words came out as a whisper.

'Speak up,' her father was always shouting at her. 'What's the matter with you? Cat got your tongue?' She often wondered where the phrase had originated. Why would a cat take someone's tongue? It seemed so unlikely.

She smiled to herself at the thought of a cat biting someone's tongue. And then she heard a voice, close beside her.

'Hello, are you alright?'

She looked up to see a soldier. His uniform told one story, his face another. His fresh skin and soft hazel eyes made her think of laughter. Yet his army jacket, spattered with something, dust perhaps, or worse; it spoke of the brutality of combat.

'I'm alright, yes.'

105

'You shouldn't sit here, it's not safe. What if there is another round of bombing? Do you live nearby? Can I see you home safe?'

'How did you know I was English?' she said.

'A guess. If you hadn't replied I would have pointed. It usually does the trick. I'm embarrassed to admit, I haven't learned many words since I've been here. *Please, thank you, water* are about my limit.' He smiled at her and she looked away, towards the church.

'I was hoping to catch a glimpse of the happy couple,' she said.

He raised an eyebrow.

'The wedding. I thought if I sat here, I might see them emerge.'

He followed her gaze.

'A car pulled up a while back. A taxi.'

'No, that can't be right. Taxis are only allowed to take the military, injured solders, VIPs.'

She smiled. 'Well, this bride was clever. She wore a soldier's cap instead of a veil. In case they got stopped, I suppose.'

'Do you know them?'

'No, nothing like that. I just think they're so brave.'

'Brave?'

'Yes, to be so certain at a time like this, when everything is fluid, constantly changing.'

'Best to grab at life, while we can.'

'Is that what you do?'

'It's all I can do. Here I am in a strange country, wearing a strange uniform, doing a job I don't really understand...'

'Fighting?'

'I'm a driver. Sure, I understand that part okay, but all

the undercurrents of war, the politics, I can't think about any of that.'

'So many people have died, it's such an endless waste. And what's it all for? Aren't we all the same? Fathers, sons, mothers, daughters, why do we have to take sides?

'It's confusing alright. Look at Italy. One minute the Italians are our enemy, the next they're fighting alongside us.'

'It's Mussolini's fault. But you're right about it being complicated. Some Italians speak of how much Mussolini has done for them, developing acres of farmland for them to grow food, the summer camps for the children. They thought he cared about the people, but then Hitler came along...'

'That's what I'm saying. The twists and turns of life, right and wrong aren't always so easy to determine.'

The bells began to sound. They both turned towards the church and a few moments later the heavy oak door opened. First to emerge was the priest, dressed in a long white cassock, with a red and gold amice, like a long scarf draped around his shoulders. The bride wore a cream suit, the tailored jacket accentuating her narrow waist. Her hair was piled up high at the back of her head, a single white flower tucked behind one ear, providing the perfect contrast to her raven black locks. She held a small posy of flowers and a small white prayer book. The groom wore the uniform of an Italian soldier. His eyes didn't leave his bride for a second, so much so he almost tripped as they walked down the church steps, hand in hand. Their two witnesses followed them down the steps. She felt sad for them, there was no confetti, no music or laughter.

'I wonder if they have a camera. Someone should take

some photos.' The young English soldier stood up. 'Ah, there, that's good.' One of the witnesses took a small camera from her handbag and started taking photos, just as the sun emerged from behind a small white cloud.

'What a wonderful scene,' he said. Now they'll always have something to remind them.'

'You don't need photos to remember things.'

'What do you remember?'

'When I close my eyes, I can see my hometown. I can see the seagulls circling over the cliffs, the white horses on the water. I can even hear the screech of the gulls and smell the fisherman's early morning catch.'

'You grew up by the coast?'

'Yes, near Tidehaven. Do you know it?'

'That's a coincidence. Yes, I know it very well. I'm from Brightport, just along the coast. How long have you lived in Anzio?'

'My father's work brought us here.'

'It must have been difficult for you. The English weren't welcome for a time.'

'I missed my friends.'

'Will you stay on here, after the war?'

'Who knows what will happen after the war. Right now, it is as though it will never end.'

'Can I see you home?'

She looked away from him, towards the little back street that ran alongside the piazza. 'Sometimes, when I'm walking around the streets I try to imagine the place as it was. Or even as it will be.'

'Without war?'

'Yes. Children enjoying an ice-cream, families strolling before supper. They call it a *passegiata.'*

'I suppose it's the weather that makes a difference.

Back home there aren't many days you can have a pleasant evening walk, even in the summer.'

'I wonder if I'll ever see my hometown again.'

'Of course you will. After the war things will be good again. I fervently believe that. But you might not want to leave all this behind. If my family was here, I might look to stay on, learn the language, marry a pretty Italian girl.' He watched her mouth as the edges moved into the beginnings of a smile.

'Now you're teasing me,' she said.

'Perhaps.'

The wedding party had moved away from the piazza, leaving a sad silence, as if they had never been.

'Will I see you again?' the soldier said. 'I mean, do you live nearby?'

She smiled.

'It's forward of me, but has anyone ever told you how beautiful you are when you smile? It's as though someone has just turned a light on.'

She tugged her hair back into a ponytail, hoping he wouldn't notice her blushing. 'You have a way with words.'

She stood, held her hand out to shake his and then moved away from the little bar. He watched her as she walked across the piazza.

Chapter 13

Easter Sunday - Bottle Alley

All the time he spoke Luigi looked away from Janie, gazing out towards the horizon. The underpass was cold and damp and Janie shivered a little, pulling her jacket tight and flipping up the collar.

'My mother remembered the English soldier as a kind, gentle person, who gave her a sense of hope.' Luigi's voice was now barely a whisper and Janie had to turn her head towards him to catch each word.

'This happened after your mother had married? After you were born?'

'I would have been about three years old. Perhaps she left me with a neighbour. There would have been no shortage of kind neighbours wanting to look after me. Italians love children.' The tone of his voice had changed, as though now he was ready to defend his mother for anything and everything she might have done all those years ago.

'Did she see the soldier again?'

He shook his head. 'She returned to the same bar several times, but he never came back.'

'I wonder if she ever told your father about the soldier.' Janie was quiet for a few moments while she turned over a few thoughts in her head and then she spoke. 'Luigi, did you hope my dad was that soldier?'

He looked directly at her, his expression wide-eyed.

'It's crazy, I know. But when I met Jessica and she told me about her brother, that he had been to Italy in the war. I thought there was a chance. Perhaps for a moment I wanted to believe in miracles.'

'She gave you no idea who the soldier was, no name?'

'Perhaps it was just a story. Perhaps she never met a soldier. You have to understand that my mother lived inside her head for much of the time.'

'It sounds as though she was lonely. It must have been difficult for her, spending so much time on her own, with your father away.'

Luigi lit another cigarette and paced backwards and forwards as he smoked.

'Did you meet Jessica soon after your mother died?' Janie was starting to see connections. For a few moments neither of them spoke.

'Are you able to tell me how she died? Was she ill for a long time, or was it sudden?'

He stopped pacing, but then started tapping one foot as though the movement would help to chase away the thoughts tumbling around his brain. 'She lost the will to go on living. She gave up hope, you see. And without hope, what do any of us have?'

'Did your mother take her own life, Luigi?' Janie used the same gentle tone she used when lulling Michelle to sleep.

He gave a brief nod in reply. 'I was the one who found her.' His head was bent low to his chest, causing Janie to struggle to capture his words as their beginnings and ends disappeared into the rollneck of his sweater.

'I can't imagine what a dreadful shock that must have been.'

'It was the day after my birthday. The evening before my mother had cooked my favourite meal. Her lasagne was better than anything in a restaurant. But it is a dish I will never taste again.'

111

'I'm sure she was a wonderful cook.'

'She had learned the Italian fervour for food. To feed someone well is to show them how much you love them. In many ways she had become Italian.'

'If she had lived in Italy since she was a girl, it would have been like home for her.'

Janie watched as he appeared to be struggling with the pictures flashing through his mind.

'If she had returned to England before the war, I would have her still,' he said, a certainty in his tone.

'You think being in Italy made her unhappy?'

'No, not Italy. My father.'

The thread of his story was muddled, all his memories and emotions a whirlwind of confusion.

'You were saying, about your birthday meal?' She tried to gently guide him back.

'My father was not there. Too busy, he told us. *We can celebrate when I come home.*' Luigi scrunched his hands into fists. 'Yes, it was a good celebration indeed. He returned to find his wife was dead and his son had left.'

'You must have wanted to blank it all out.'

'I left my father a note. I told him my mother's death was his fault and that I would never forgive him.' His face contorted. The handsome face that must have turned the heads of many Italian signorinas now seemed almost ugly.

'Where did you go?'

'I stayed with Mario, he is a good friend. I knew my father would never find me there. He doesn't know my friends, he knows nothing about me.'

'It must have been such a lonely time.' She touched his shoulder and felt him trembling.

'It was easier being alone. Mario was at work most of

112

the time. I slept a lot, drank a lot. Too much.' He stopped speaking and looked down at a pile of sand and tiny pebbles that had been thrown up from the last high tide. He bent down, picked up some of the sand, then let it trickle through his fingers, back to the ground.

'Mario must be a good friend.'

'Yes, he is the best of friends. I spent a few weeks not going out, not doing anything, then one day he told me I had to stop hiding, he made me face life again.'

'What did you do for money?'

'Mario offered me a job in his bar.'

'And then you met Jessica?'

'You know the rest.' He threw the cigarette butt down on the ground. Then he stood and stretched, rising to his full height, pulling his shoulders back, as though he was reinforcing his position in the world.

'Come on, let's go back now. Dad and Jessica will be wondering where we've got to. And Greg and I are due round my in-laws for tea. If we're late I'll never hear the end of it.'

They started walking back towards the beginning of *Bottle Alley*, Janie pushing the pram and Luigi walking in silence beside her.

'Thank you for telling me about your mother. Talking about it all again can't have been easy.'

'You're easy to talk to.'

'And Jessica?'

'I don't have anything to hide.'

Janie got the feeling that Luigi had answered another question entirely.

'There's more I need to tell you,' he said. It was as though he had opened the tap to his memories and now they were flooding out. 'The night my mother died I got very drunk. I worked my way through my dad's wine cellar, then I went into my father's study, ransacked his desk. I was convinced my father had a mistress. I couldn't imagine anyone would devote so much of their life to business alone. There had to be a woman at the heart of it. I was certain I would find something, a photo, a love letter.'

'Do you think your mother suspected your father was having an affair. Was that why she was so unhappy.'

Luigi fixed his gaze on Janie, but it was as though he was looking straight through her, to another place, another time. 'I'll never know. The hardest thing to bear is that I can't talk to her and she didn't feel she could talk to me.'

'She wanted to protect you. It's natural for a mother to want to protect her child.'

For a moment, Janie's thoughts went to her daughter. She bent over the pram, smiling at Michelle, who responded by waving her arms around, her hands curled into tiny fists. Then she refocused on Luigi, who was wiping tears from his face. 'You've been through a lot. It's been hard for you. And your friendship with Jessica? Were you hoping she could help?'

'You think I have used your aunt, don't you?' Luigi's tone was accusatory, it seemed his emotions were quick to change from grief to anger, then back to grief again.

'Jessica knows her own mind. It's not for me to say.'

'I saw the chance for a pilgrimage.'

Janie gave him a questioning look and waited for him to continue.

'Coming here to England, to the south coast, it was a chance to find out more about my mother, who she was before...'

'Before she went to Italy?'

'Before she lost her way. That is where I was the evening Bertie died. I walked and thought of my mother.'

'Imagining her old haunts?'

'Yes. She would have walked the seafront, even played on the beach. I like to hold the pebbles, to pretend they were the same ones she held.'

He held his empty hands out towards Janie, as though he was showing her the beachstones.

'We could ask around,' Janie said, a lift in her voice, 'find out if anyone remembers the family. My good friend, Phyllis Frobisher, has lived here her whole life. She may even remember your mother.'

'You want to help. I know that. I thought being here would bring me closer to my mother's memory, instead it is like a tree with no roots, all it can do is topple and fall.'

'And now with Bertie's death?'

'I'll do what you ask. I will ring my father.'

'I'm confused. When we spoke before you told me you thought your father sent Bertie here to follow you. But just now you told me a different story.'

He gave a wry smile. 'I can see why you are an investigator.'

'I'm sure your father will want to help you. If he knows the police have taken your passport, he will want help clear your name.'

'Before I left England, I wrote to my father again. I told him I was coming here. I told him about your aunt and said she had helped me more in a few months than he had ever done in my lifetime.'

Janie said nothing, but had a passing image of Luigi's father and the pain that the letter must have caused him.

115

'You think I am without heart, without feeling,' he said, glaring at her.

She went to shake her head, to reply, but he spoke again. 'My heart was broken when my mother died, so perhaps you are right.'

Throughout the hour or so Janie spent at her in-laws' house she kept revisiting the conversation she had had with Luigi. The story he had told her was sad and yet in some ways she was relieved to have heard it. The build-up of black marks on Luigi's character now seemed to have dissipated. Yes, he had behaved strangely, but now she could understand some of the reasons for his actions. A couple of times she was so immersed in her thoughts that Nell Juke had to repeat a question before Janie realised anyone was speaking.

'Don't forget to take the cardigans,' Nell said, laying Michelle on her lap and inspecting her outfit. 'I've knitted the second size but she'll have outgrown that in no time. You are sure you're not feeding her too often? She seems to have filled out since we saw her just last week. Babies like a routine, you shouldn't let her dictate to you.'

'It's fine, mum,' Greg replied, before Janie could speak.

'All these new-fangled ideas of feeding on demand,' Nell said, 'I don't hold with it. You have to set boundaries. That's what we did with Greg and Rebecca and it never did them any harm.'

'Mum, really, you mustn't worry. Janie and I know what we're doing.'

Back home later that evening, Janie settled Michelle for the evening, then flopped down on the sofa and put her feet up on Greg's lap.

'Foot massage do the trick? It's been a long day, hasn't it?' Greg said.

'Long weekend, more like. It's ironic, isn't it? I couldn't wait for Jessica to get back from Italy, instead it's been nothing but dramas since she arrived.'

'Not her fault, though.'

'No, definitely not her fault. Except maybe her choice of friends.'

'Luigi?'

'He's a pretty troubled soul, isn't he?'

'The story he told me today, it was just so sad.'

'And he thought your dad was that English soldier?'

Janie closed her eyes, laying her head back onto one of the cushions. 'I suppose he thought he might find something in dad's bedroom, a photo or a little keepsake.'

'It's a long shot, though isn't it? I don't think he can have really imagined he'd find the soldier. Seems to me he lives in a dream world.'

'Losing your mum like that, well it would screw you up, wouldn't it?'

'Suicide is pretty grim. You'd have to be more than miserable to take your own life.'

'Do you think he blames his dad?'

'He said his parents didn't get on, that all his father is interested in is his work. He seems pretty bitter about the whole thing.'

'He would be. Anyone would be. Imagine how you would be if your dad died.'

'It would be unbearable. I'd be devastated. But I wouldn't be angry.'

'Grief can make people feel all sorts of emotions.'

'I'm surprised he didn't tell Jessica.'

'Some men don't find it easy to open up.'

Janie sat up and put her arm around her husband, pulling him close to her. 'You'll always tell me, won't you?'

'Tell you what?'

'If you're upset about something? If you're worried, or sad?'

'Right now the only thing I'm worried about is that you're thinking this is another case for you to solve. You've got yourself into a state and you're imagining all sorts.'

'I'm not imagining anything, Greg, I'm just telling you what he told me.'

'What do you think is going on then?'

'I have no idea, but something is not quite right.'

There were still unanswered questions in Janie's mind. If she could discover the reason for Bertie's visit to Tamarisk Bay, perhaps she could make more sense of it all. And then there was Rosetta. There was something odd about her behaviour. Of course, she was upset about finding a dead body in one of her guest bedrooms, but Janie was sure there was something else going on. Could it be linked to the Denaros, or to Rosetta's Italian connections?

'Okay, enough now,' Greg said, 'I can hear your mind whirring. I'm going to put the telly on and make us a hot drink and then I think we should open your Easter egg.'

There was more than one house in Tamarisk Bay where Easter had had to fade into the background.

Frank Bright slumped down into the fireside chair, kicking off his slippers and stretching out his toes towards the coal fire.

'Luke and Tom asleep at last?' he said, watching his

wife folding a pile of clean nappies. 'You going to relax for five minutes?'

'I need to do your sandwiches and put the dirty nappies to soak.'

'Leave it a while, Nikki, you look exhausted. Come and sit with me, we've hardly had the chance to talk for days.' Frank pulled his wife down to sit on his lap and folded his arms around her.

'You must be tired too, it's been one late night after another and all over a bank holiday weekend.'

'Crime doesn't stop for holidays. In fact, just the opposite in my experience.'

'You're worried about this case, aren't you?'

'I worry about all of them.'

'I know you do. But I can tell when there's one that gets under your skin. I can see it in your face. And you've been so restless in the night.'

'You should know. With those boys of ours, you barely get an hour's sleep most nights.'

'I know. But it won't be forever. It'll be easier in a few months, they'll slip into a routine.' She searched his face. 'Talk to me,' she said.

'There's been a death.' As he spoke he shuffled the facts around in his mind.

'A murder in Tamarisk Bay, no wonder you're all fired up.'

'I don't know if it's murder. That's the problem.'

'Please don't tell me it's someone we know.' Nikki searched his face for clues.

'No, nothing like that. But your friend is involved again.'

Nikki drew in a sharp breath.

'Janie Juke.' Frank's tone was sharp.

'We're not friends anymore. Not really.'

'I shouldn't be talking about it to you. I shouldn't be talking about it all. Forget I mentioned it.'

'I'm hardly going to do that now. I'm guessing Janie is making things difficult for you.'

'Yes and no. She likes digging around, asking questions.'

'And that's your job.'

'If I'm completely honest she does have a knack for it.'

'Some people don't like talking to the police.'

'You could be right there.'

'Don't let her get under your skin, but make the most of her. If people are telling her things they won't tell you then make her your ally. You don't have to be on opposite sides.'

Planting a kiss on his wife's cheek, Frank took her left hand in his and touched her wedding ring. 'I knew there was a reason I married you.'

Chapter 14

Easter Monday - the Juke household

Easter Monday arrived with the very best of spring. As soon as the sun was up it filled the Juke house with bright rays, casting patches of light and shade over the furniture. Unfortunately, it also showed up the dust and a few fine cobwebs in the higher corners of the kitchen. Ignoring the mental list of household chores that Janie had been rehearsing since she woke in the early hours, she wrapped Michelle in an extra blanket, put a jacket over her own dressing gown and stepped out into the back garden.

The crocuses and snowdrops that had broken through the frosty ground several weeks earlier had finishing their flowering. By way of compensation a large clump of daffodils had sprung up in the far corner of the garden, under the shelter of a beech tree.

Standing for a few minutes on the back doorstep, Janie watched a few small birds jostling each other for access to the bird table. The day before she had refilled both the bird feeders, but now they were almost empty. She guessed the squirrels would have had their share, but then nature had its own way of resolving power struggles. She smiled at the memory of conversations with her friend, Zara, who passionately supported animals over humans.

'Maybe you'll meet Zara one day,' she whispered to her daughter. 'She opened my eyes to many things, injustice being one. Maybe we have injustices going on here again, what do you think?' As if she understood every word, Michelle opened her eyes wide and made a little chattering noise.

'Are you talking to yourself?' Greg sidled up to his wife. He was bundled in his dressing gown, his early morning stubble and half-closed eyes, making him look more asleep than awake.

'I'm warning our daughter about some of the problems in the world.'

'A touch early for such serious discussions.'

'In the day, or in her life?'

'Both. Come on back inside. It might be sunny, but it's still cold.'

Greg had just put the kettle on the gas when the doorbell rang.

'You have to be kidding. Surely the milkman isn't expecting to collect his money on a Bank Holiday.' Greg tightened the cord around his dressing gown and opened the front door.

'Morning.' Libby stood on the doorstep, her chic blonde bob and neatly pencilled eye makeup a sharp contrast to Greg's dishevelled appearance. 'I come bearing gifts.' She pushed past Greg and made her way through to the kitchen. 'Hot cross buns.' Without waiting for a reply, she opened one of the kitchen cupboards and pulled out a baking tray. 'Shall I put the oven on while you make the drinks?'

'Don't jiggle her too much, she's not long had a feed.' Janie had just one focus as Libby took Michelle and lifted her high in the air, then started to waltz around the kitchen table.

'What's the low-down on the new man in town, Michelle?' Libby said, slowing to a stop and moving Michelle so her head was resting on Libby's shoulder.

'What makes you so bright and breezy at this

ridiculously early hour and who are you on about?' Janie said.

'Mr Romeo. Jessica's *friend.*' Libby emphasised the word with a wide-eyed grin. 'Is he gorgeous? Those Latin looks, oh, I can just imagine.'

Greg had been standing in the kitchen doorway and now that he could guess where the conversation was headed he was keen to escape. 'I need to finish getting ready. I'll leave you girls to it, but please don't corrupt my daughter with your talking. Remember, all that glitters isn't gold.'

'What's glitter got to do with it?' Libby asked.

'Just because someone's got good looks, it doesn't always mean he's a good catch. I don't want Michelle to get the wrong idea,' Greg called out as he climbed the stairs.

'Is he then? Good looking, I mean?' Libby grabbed a muslin cloth from Janie as Michelle brought up the last of her milk over Libby's jacket. 'Oh, delightful. Thank you. Couldn't you have waited until I'd handed you back to your mother? That's no way to treat my newest acquisition, it took me two months to save up for it and then I only managed to afford it in the January sales.'

'I did warn you, here let me sponge it clean for you. Sit down and hold my daughter still for a minute. You've got far too much energy for this time of the morning. How many coffees have you had?'

With drinks made, regurgitated milk cleaned up and Greg snatching a few moments of peace in the back garden, the girls moved into the sitting room.

'I'd hate to hear what Ray has to say when he finds out you're pining over some stranger.' Janie picked a currant from one of the hot cross buns and rolled it around in her fingers.

'What he doesn't know can't hurt him. And are you going to eat that, or just play with it?'

'This weekend has taken the edge off my appetite to be honest. Are you two okay?'

'Ray and me? Of course, why shouldn't we be? But just because I'm happy with steak and kidney pie doesn't mean I can't drool over the occasional knickerbocker glory.'

'You're incorrigible.'

'Thank you. I'll take that as a compliment.'

'Well, yes, Luigi is good-looking, if dark, swarthy and continental is your thing.'

'Sounds delicious.'

'But like Greg says, it's not all about looks.'

'Why, does he have a wicked secret past? And what did I miss that's put you off your food?'

Janie arranged the cushions in one corner of the settee, laid Michelle against them and spent the next ten minutes filling Libby in on the events of the past few days.

'Oh, my God. I missed it all for a stupid dance, which wasn't even all that good. I could have been on the scene, filed a first-hand report. I might have even got a front-page lead.'

'Libby, a man died. This isn't about your missed opportunities for a scoop and a bonus from your editor.'

'I know, I know. So, if DS Bright has interviewed all of you he must believe there's more to it.'

Janie twisted her empty cup around on its saucer, replaying the last couple of days' events before replying. 'There's more to it, yes. I'm certain of it. But what that *more* is, I have no idea.'

'Let's think it through. Remember you and I are the best investigative brains in Tamarisk Bay. We solved the last mystery we worked on together, so let's do it again.'

'Tracking down a missing person is one thing, but this time there's a dead body.'

'Oh, come on, what's stopping you? Poirot would be in there like a shot.'

'Libby, this is serious.'

'And so are we. Come on, where's your notebook? I'll watch the baby while you fetch it. I promise not to shake her about. We'll just sit here quietly together. But be quick, I'll have to leave for work soon.'

'You're working on a Bank Holiday?'

'News doesn't stop for holidays, you know.'

'Okay, you go to work, then call back here later, when you've finished. In the meantime, I'll jot down a few notes and we can look at them together.'

'Sounds like a plan.'

'And don't forget, you can't mention anything I've told you to your editor, or I'll end up being arrested.'

'There's nothing illegal about reporting a local death in a local paper, surely?'

Later that day, Janie and Libby left Greg watching a Brian Rix farce on television, while they scanned through Janie's notes.

'Okay, so talk me through it again and focus on the areas where you have your doubts,' Libby said.

'I have my doubts about the whole thing.'

'Come on, focus.' A slight note of impatience crept into Libby's voice.

'Okay, so first thing - why did Bertie come here to Tamarisk Bay? And it seems like he was on the same train as Luigi.'

'That's two things.'

'I know, but they're connected. Then we have the shirt with blood that Luigi stuffed under his bed.'

'Maybe he's just very untidy. One of these men who throws his dirty clothes on the floor and forgets about them. It's not like Bertie had a knife sticking in him when you found him.'

'This is no time for jokes. It's weird about the briefcase too. Plus, the police have taken Luigi's passport.'

'So, the briefcase the police took from Bertie's room was definitely not Luigi's?'

'He says it wasn't.'

'Focus on the facts. We know that Alberto and Bertie are business associates. Perhaps Bertie was genuinely here on business and it's just pure coincidence Luigi arrived at the same time, on the same train. But I've found out some interesting stuff from Marcus - he's my editor. He's really interested in international politics.'

'What's he doing working on a local rag, then?'

'Needs must, I suppose. He's got a young family. Anyway, that's not important. What is important is that he knows a lot about what's been going on in Italy.'

Janie raised an eyebrow and waited for her friend to continue.

'I had a long talk to him today.'

'Libby, please tell me you haven't spilt the beans about Bertie's death. It'll only get me into trouble with DS Bright. He'll know the story came from me and I'll be Mrs Unpopular - again.'

'Don't panic. I didn't breathe a word. I just pretended to have developed an interest. I told him how important it was for me to have an overview of world affairs if I wanted to advance my career.'

'Sounds plausible.'

'It must have been because he fell for it and spent nearly an hour explaining all the ins and outs of what's been going on in Europe since the Second World War - from a political perspective. To be honest the majority of it went straight over my head.'

'But you learned something useful? About Italy?'

'Yes, exactly that. I steered him away from the wider overview and asked him about Italy specifically. I said I've always had a fascination for the country.'

'So what did you find out that can help us with the death of an English stranger in an Italian-run guest house?'

'When you put it like that I suppose it all sounds a bit crazy. But basically it's all to do with the Mafia.'

'What is?'

'The Mafia has control over loads of state organisations in Italy.'

'And businesses?'

'Definitely.'

'It seems that over the last decade or more there's been a huge rise in organised crime and violence in Italy and the authorities have tracked it all back to the Mafia. Five or six years ago there was a massive round up, hundreds of people were arrested and charged with all sorts, drug trafficking, even murder.' Libby paused to allow the effect of her words to sink in, then she continued. 'The trials are ongoing but there's evidence to link them to brutal killings, even the death of policemen.'

'This is all fascinating, but I can't see how any of it has any relevance to Bertie, or Luigi for that matter.'

'I thought you were the one with the detective's mind.

Poirot would not be impressed. Think about it for a minute. What if Bertie has committed a crime, tax evasion or worse and he knows something that implicates Luigi's father. That would be enough reason for Mr Denaro to make sure Bertie was silenced. Maybe he organised a hit on him? Perhaps he knew too much?'

Janie ran her fingers through her hair and sighed. 'You've read too many crime novels and watched too many thrillers.'

Libby jumped up from the armchair and thrust her hands in front of Janie's face, tapping one finger at a time as she counted. 'One - we need to find out more about Bertie. Two - we need to speak to Luigi and ask him what he knows about his dad's business affairs and three ...'

'Slow down. I know how excited you get once you're on a mission. All you can see is your chance for a big, bold headline, '*Mafia trail leads to death in Tamarisk Bay*' with Libby Frobisher getting a nice exclusive and another pat on the back from your boss. But it's not going to be that easy.'

Janie was standing now and holding her hand out she mimicked her friend's actions. 'One - Bertie is dead, so he's not going to tell us a thing. Two - Luigi's relationship with his dad is bordering on non-existent, so I'm doubtful he'll co-operate, leaving us exactly nowhere. Meanwhile, I've got Jessica feeling guilty about bringing Luigi here in the first place and Rosetta being completely paranoid about the reputation of her guest house.'

'Oh, bless her. Yes, I'd forgotten Rosetta. She's had a rough time of it, hasn't she.'

'She's so anti police. She must have had a dreadful run-in with them at some point in her past.'

'Another mystery there?'

Janie smiled and wagged her finger. 'Oh, no you don't. We've got enough to deal with just now, without looking for even more to investigate.'

'Okay, listen, I've had an idea.'

'It always worries me when you say that.'

'But this is a good one.'

'And...?' Janie lent her head to one side and waited.

'I haven't met Luigi yet. How about you introduce me to him and let me see what I can get out of him. A different approach might do the trick?'

'And Ray won't mind you spending time with another bloke? A dishy Italian at that?'

Libby's face broke into a broad smile. 'He'll understand, especially if I promise to make it up to him.'

'No, this time it's down to me. But if you'd like to be my sounding board, then drop back round in a day or so and I'll update you.'

'Good luck then.'

'Thanks, I'll need it.'

Chapter 15

Tuesday morning - Tamarisk Bay

Janie opened her wardrobe and rifled through the array of dresses and skirts. Today was the day she planned to discover whether she could fit back into her favourite mini dress. For months she'd floated about in oversized smocks and maternity dresses and for the first few weeks after Michelle was born it still seemed as though she would never get her slim figure back. Every chance she had she'd been doing the exercises the health visitor had suggested. The only trouble was if Greg caught her doing them he teased her relentlessly, until they both dissolved into giggles.

She pulled a red woollen shift dress from its hanger and held it up against her, admiring herself in the mirror.

'Should be okay,' she muttered to herself, before throwing her nightie on top of the pile of washing that laid on the bedroom floor, ready to be carried down to the kitchen. Then she dressed, breathing in a little as she tried to close the zip that ran up one side of the dress. Twisting two scarves into a plait she created a red and white headband, which she eased over her hair, tucking her fringe back. Just one rogue strand seemed determined to escape. Dressing Michelle in a white Babygro and a red cardigan, she stood in front of the mirror again with her daughter in her arms.

'What a pair we make. Come on let's go and wow your great-aunt. Show her we can hold our own when it comes to fancy continental fashion.'

As if in response, Michelle grabbed at Janie's hair, tugging at it until Janie prised her fingers apart.

It was a day for clothes.

'Fancy a spot of clothes shopping?' Jessica asked, as Janie let herself in the front door. 'Travelling light is all well and good, but it means I need a constant restocking of my wardrobe.'

'Sounds good to us, doesn't it, Michelle?' Janie peered into the pram to see if her daughter had woken up.

'Don't think boutiques, though. My shopping is strictly confined to charity shops.'

'My guess is you'll have plenty to choose from,' Philip chipped in, as he walked into the hallway to greet his daughter.

'Clothes or shops?' Jessica asked.

'Both.' Philip and Janie answered simultaneously, making all three laugh, which in turn ensured that Michelle woke up.

Tamarisk Bay was busy with holidaymakers. Couples down from London for the Easter weekend, young families determined to spend the school holidays at the seaside, regardless of the weather. *The Haven* caravan park, situated between Tamarisk Bay and Brightport was usually full during the holiday season. Janie had worked there for a couple of summer seasons behind the bar when she was in her late teens. In-between clearing tables and washing glasses she liked watching the local boys hovering around the edge of the dance floor, waiting for the slow dances and a chance to meet a girl from out of town. After she met Greg she'd teased him about it.

'Don't tell me you weren't tempted. A quick kiss, then they head off home and you're being chased by the next starry-eyed girl dreaming of a holiday romance.'

'That doesn't even deserve an answer and I've only got eyes for you.'

'Ah, you say all the right things.'

'What are you smiling about?' Jessica brought Janie back to the present as they waited at the zebra crossing for a car to stop.

'Did you and dad used to hang around *The Haven* when you were teenagers?'

'It wasn't there when we were teenagers - you forget what a couple of old cronies we are.'

'Rubbish. Tell you what, how about we go up there one day, I'll show you around. You'll love it. But first we need to sort out this business with Luigi. The police have taken his passport, it's not looking good for him.'

'The more time I spend with him, the more of an enigma he seems to be. Although enigma probably isn't the right word, it sounds too light-hearted and right now all that's happened since we arrived has been just the opposite.'

Once they crossed onto the seafront, Janie gestured to Jessica to take hold of the pram. Sharing what she now knew about her aunt's friend would be easier without worrying about weaving around oncoming walkers and cyclists. The seafront was busier than usual; the unexpected sunshine bringing out a crowd keen to make the most of it.

'Jessica, Luigi told me a really sad story yesterday.'

Her aunt stopped pushing the pram and turned to face Janie, then they continued walking while Janie told her aunt about Eloise, and the soldier and all that Luigi had shared with her.

'I had no idea. No wonder he's been struggling. Sitting on the outside of a family reunion when your own family life is in tatters would really mess with your head. I feel terrible that he's had so much sadness to cope with and he wasn't able to talk to me. But I'll admit, I've never been good with all of that.'

'It's probably easier because he doesn't know me.'

'You don't judge, that encourages openness.'

'Neither do you.'

'Live and let live, that's my motto.'

Jessica was quiet for a few moments and then she said, 'it seems dreadful to be out shopping, knowing what he's been going through. And then his father's friend dies and the police start treating him like he's a suspect. He must feel as though he's in the middle of a nightmare he can't wake up from. You don't think he's done anything wrong, Janie, do you?'

'I'm keeping an open mind. I don't think he's a murdered, if that's what you're thinking.'

'Dear God, what a terrible thing. I should never have agreed when he asked to come to England with me. I don't know what I was thinking. To be honest I wasn't thinking. I've got so used to drifting along wherever life takes me.'

A few minutes later they reached the Oxfam shop, which nestled between a record shop and a greengrocer's, half-way up London Road.

'Drifting is good, for now let's enjoy our shopping trip. They'll be time enough to help Luigi, but first he needs to accept that he needs help.' Janie said, as she helped Jessica negotiate the pram over the door threshold. 'That might be as tricky as this door threshold.'

Jessica took her time, wandering around the clothes

section of the shop, sliding hangers across the metal rails, selecting various garments to look at more closely. She picked out a black and white checked mini dress, holding it up against her. She flicked back her hair and moved into a pose, her own Indian cotton dress showing below the hemline of the sixties style mini.

'You remind me of those paper dolls I used to play with as a child,' Janie said. 'Do you remember? I used to cut the outfits out and then fold back the little paper tabs and attach them to the dolls.'

'Oh, I remember alright. You were always parading them in front of me. One of your favourites was, *Look, Auntie, my doll is going horse-riding.* And I remember the time when you dressed one of them as a bride, in a beautiful long white dress, with bright red shoes. *Isn't she gorgeous, Auntie?* I didn't have the heart to tell you about the shoes.'

'And what was wrong with a bride wearing red shoes, anyway?' Janie laughed.

Jessica moved over to the next rail and pulled out another dress, ankle length and seersucker material, with its background shades of burnt orange blending perfectly with the auburn hues of her hair.

'Perfect,' Janie said.

'It reminds me of Siena. I must take you there one day. It's the most beautiful of all the cities I've visited.'

'More beautiful than Rome?'

'It's something to do with the light. No wonder artists love it.'

'You should be an artist. I can imagine you in a smock with a smudge of paint across your cheek.' Janie pressed her hand up to her aunt's cheek. 'It's so good to have you here, I've missed you.'

'You haven't had time to miss me. Do you know when I first walked through the door at your dad's house and saw you standing there, it sounds funny to say it now, but you took my breath away; confident, stylish, beautiful.'

'Hardly beautiful. That's why I dress my hair up with scarves and headbands, it adds a bit of spice to my otherwise mousy locks.'

'There's nothing mousy about you. Wife, mother, librarian, successful sleuth. You haven't let anything hold you back and I'm proud of you. Your dad is too.'

'Do you think he's okay?'

'Your dad? Of course, more than okay.'

'But he doesn't have many adventures.'

'Living vicariously can be fun. You keep him amused with your antics.'

'But what about love? Maybe he misses mum? Or maybe he wishes he could replace her?'

'Your dad is fine. We've had some good chats since I've been back. He loves being a grandad, having Michelle around is like having a miniature you. And you know what a brilliant physiotherapist he is. Anyway, you don't always need other people to make you complete. Sometimes the most precious times are when you can close the door on the world and listen to music, or just dream, undisturbed. He's got Charlie too, remember.'

'Thanks, Jessica.'

'You don't need to thank me. I'll always be there for you and for your dad. Even when I'm travelling, I'm never more than a few hours away.'

They left the Oxfam shop, Jessica having handed over a few shillings for two kaftans, as well as the orange dress she had modelled earlier, and made their way to *Jefferson's*.

Janie had promised to buy the coffees, provided Jessica shared a few of the juicier snippets from her travelling adventures.

'Come on, tell me about your love life. Luigi wasn't your first boyfriend, I bet.'

Jessica stopped pushing the pram and turned to her niece. 'Luigi is *just* a friend.'

Once inside the café, Janie gave Richie their order and joined Jessica at an empty table that had enough space for the pram. Jessica grabbed another chair and loaded her shopping bags onto it.

'Okay, so who else did you captivate? A few Greek gods and Spanish Lotharios?' Janie said, pulling back the pram's covers. The café was steamy, the smell of cigarette smoke mingling with the smells of fried bacon. Richie approached their table with two mugs of coffee, putting them down on the table, before extending his hand towards Jessica. 'And you are...?'

'Janie's Aunt Jessica,' she said, shaking his hand and smiling when he held onto hers for a little longer than necessary.

'Ah, yes, the elusive adventurer. Now it all makes sense.'

Jessica raised an eyebrow, tipping her head to one side, waiting for him to expand.

'Your niece is forever waving postcards around, telling us about your travels to far-flung countries, making us all jealous when we're coping with another grey day in Tamarisk Bay.'

'Richie has had to put up with my moaning since Christmas.' Janie jiggled the handle of the pram to settle her daughter's grumbles.

'It's nice to be missed,' Jessica said.

'I for one, hope you are here for a while.' Richie half turned on hearing the tinkle of the doorbell, indicating the arrival of another customer.

'Who knows? I'm not a great one for planning,' Jessica replied, but Richie had already moved away, returning to the counter to take an order from the new arrival.

Michelle's grumbles were now steadily rising in pitch, causing Jessica to look into the pram. 'Is she hungry?'

'She shouldn't be, not quite yet, anyway. I expect she wants a cuddle. Come here, gorgeous girl.' Janie lifted her daughter out of the pram. 'We're having a girly chat and you want to be part of it, don't you?' Michelle responded by changing her grumbling noises into gurgles that could easily have been mistaken for unintelligible chatter. 'Ah, see, she's joining in. Come on then. Boyfriends? Give us the low down.'

'There have been a few, but no-one serious. Except Andreas. He mistakenly thought I might be the marrying kind.'

'You had a proposal? Weren't you tempted?'

'Oh, don't get me wrong. Living in a Greek village, waving him off in his fishing boat each morning, a goat for milking in the front yard and a donkey in the back. Picking handfuls of wild oregano and lemons from our own trees. Yes, for a moment. But there was too much to give up.'

'Like what?'

'If I'd said yes, I'd never have gone to Italy. As soon as you take one fork in the road, it's so much harder to go into reverse and explore the other one.'

'Do you think I should have waited to see what the other fork in my road had in store for me?'

Jessica smiled, laying her hand on Michelle, who was now starting to doze in Janie's arms. 'What, and miss out on this angel? Not likely.'

'And Luigi?'

'Italian men are all children. Their mothers keep them that way.'

'So he was looking for someone to mother him and you fell for it?'

'I didn't fall for anything. I keep telling you, we've only ever been friends. In fact, acquaintances would be a better description, especially given all that I didn't know about him.'

'He will have had his reasons for not telling you about his mum. Maybe it was just too soon to talk about it when you first met. And then later...well maybe he didn't know how to start the conversation.'

'All he told me was that she was English and I thought that was why we connected. He found out I came from the south coast. He'd always wanted to see it and hey presto. It made sense for him to come with me to visit. I honestly never thought there was anything sinister in it.'

'What about now? Now you know the truth.' Janie watched her aunt's expression and wondered if she had said too much.

'You think he's been using me? With some strange ulterior motive?'

'Why didn't he come to England on his own, years ago. He's not a child.'

Jessica gave a drawn-out sigh. 'Let's change the subject, shall we. I don't know all the ins and outs.'

'You love lost causes, don't you?'

'Do I?'

'You put your life on hold to help dad bring me up. Then, you end up looking after other people's children, other families. Didn't you ever want a family of your own?'

'Your life has followed a traditional pattern. Fall in love, get married, have a baby. Great. It works for you. I've had a different sort of life, but for me it's been perfect. I've had freedom, to travel, to make friends, then to leave them behind to make space for new friends, new experiences. I love my life just as it is.'

Jessica paused to take a breath and Janie stood up, sidled over to the other side of the table and put her arms around her aunt. 'Give me a hug. I'm pleased you're happy, that you've found a way of life that suits you. I worry you might be taken advantage of; there are unscrupulous people out there.'

'And you think Luigi is one?'

'I don't know, I'm reserving judgement.'

'Fetch us fresh coffees and then it's my turn to ask the questions.'

Janie lay her daughter back down in the pram and waited.

'Do you miss the library?' Jessica focused her gaze on Janie.

'I miss the people and the chat. But Michelle and I try to call in once a week to get all the gossip from Phyllis. Well, not gossip exactly. I don't think Phyllis would approve.'

'Phyllis Frobisher. Now there's a name that hasn't popped into my head for years.'

'She was your English teacher too, wasn't she?'

'Phyllis must have taught English to the whole of Tamarisk Bay. She must have been at that school for

forty years or more. I expect that's why she's learned not
to gossip. When you know families as well as she does
you're bound to know a few secrets.'

'We could drop round her house when we leave here if
you like.'

'Sounds perfect, yes, I'd love to see her.'

Chapter 16

Tuesday morning - Lavender Cottage

The library van did its rounds on Mondays, Wednesdays and Fridays and since Janie had to relinquish the reins for a few months, Phyllis had stepped back into a role that was hers after retirement from the local school. On any other day of the week Phyllis would be found at home, baking, or gardening, or occasionally resting with a good book.

Lavender Cottage nestled in a narrow street in the heart of Tidehaven Old Town. Arriving at the cottage, Jessica and Janie found Phyllis in the front garden, tying in the trailing clematis to a piece of string that was cleverly threaded between nails battered into the front wall of the house to form a trellis.

'Jessica Chandler. Now there's a welcome surprise. Come on in. Janie, be a love and pop the kettle on, but first let me have a cuddle with my god-daughter.'

Janie passed Michelle into Phyllis' arms and for a moment all three women gazed at the baby's face. Janie was the first to speak. 'Michelle Juke, you are a time waster. You know, Greg and I are forever watching her. It's a competition to see who will catch her first smile.'

'Don't take any notice of them, Michelle,' Phyllis said, 'you keep them waiting.'

With a pot of tea made and the biscuit tin poised on a footstool so that each could dip their hand in, Phyllis quizzed Jessica about her travels.

'And you were loath to leave in the end?'

Jessica paused before answering, casting a questioning

look at Phyllis.

'You were going to be here for Christmas. Janie regaled me with all the details of meals planned and presents chosen.'

'I know and I feel bad about that, but my plans changed.'

'So now Christmas meals have been converted into Easter fare?'

'Something like that,' Janie said.

Phyllis waited, her gaze going from one to the other. 'Has something happened?'

'With your intuition you should have joined the police force rather than the teaching profession,' Janie said.

'Oh, don't you worry, my intuition was put to good use, detecting all sorts of crimes.'

'Hiding sweets in our desks, cribbing someone else's homework?' Jessica said.

'And I seem to recall you were guilty of both on several occasions.' Phyllis smiled. 'Now what is it you're not telling me?'

'There's been a death, at Rosetta's guest house,' Janie said.

'Oh, that poor woman. All that trouble with Hugh and now this. Who died?'

'Rosetta invited us round for supper on Good Friday evening and that's when it happened.'

'Not food poisoning, I hope? She would never forgive herself if her trademark spaghetti with meatballs finished someone off.'

Jessica smiled. 'No, the poor man hadn't had a chance to eat anything. We were waiting for him before we started supper and when he didn't turn up, Rosetta went up to his room and found him.'

'Heart attack?'

'We're guessing it must have been.' Janie topped all the cups up from the teapot, adding milk and spilling some on the tray. 'But then the police turned up and interrogated us all.'

'Boot, other foot?' Phyllis said, pointedly.

Janie and Jessica cast questioning looks at her.

'The investigator becomes the investigated.'

While they finished their tea and made good inroads into the biscuit tin, Janie told Phyllis a little more about the conversations she'd had with Luigi since Good Friday evening. Phyllis listened, nodding occasionally. Then she suggested they move out into the back garden. 'I've planted up some pots, come and see what you think. I might enlist your help to move them for me. Don't get old, Jessica, it's very limiting.'

'If I can be half as fit as you when I get to your age, I'll be a very happy bunny,' Jessica said, lifting Michelle from the pram.

'Aren't you going to put a bonnet on the little one's head?' Phyllis said. 'It might be April, but it's still chilly.'

'I like people to see her curls,' Janie said, ruffling Michelle's hair through her fingers. 'Greg's mum hasn't stopped knitting, but honestly she's got more hats than days of the week. Nell is forever presenting us with another layette, cardigans, mittens. It comes to something when my daughter has a more extensive wardrobe than I do.'

'You'd better get used to it. Once she's a teenager she'll be pinching your clothes. Or maybe you'll be pinching hers,' Phyllis said, chuckling. 'So, Jessica, did you find any place to compare with Tamarisk Bay?'

'They all compared, some favourably, some not so.'

'And you had your favourites?'

Jessica stirred her drink and looked away from Phyllis, as she shuffled through the pictures in her mind.

'For different reasons. Spain was wild, dancing, music, fiestas most days that ran into most nights. The Greeks live a beautifully simple life, all focused on family. They live on the produce of the land and the bounty from the sea.'

'Didn't you join a commune at one point? You mentioned it in one of your postcards,' Janie asked.

'It wasn't really a commune, just a bunch of us looking out for each other and having fun.'

'Admit it, you were a sixties chick,' Janie said, smiling.

'Ha, not so much of a chick. I was a late starter, some of the crowd I hung out with were barely out of their teens. At thirty I was virtually the elder statesman, but it didn't stop me having fun.'

'Sounds idyllic,' Phyllis said. 'Did you see much of Italy? I had the chance to visit in the early fifties. They were struggling to recover from the war, like we all were. But the people still had their love of life, that's what struck me about them. Those feasts they have, everyone sat around a huge wooden table, sharing food and endlessly laughing. Those meals went on for hours. It makes me feel quite nostalgic thinking about it now.'

'I know what you mean. The Italians love to chat, so everywhere you go, to the bank, the post office, the butchers, you learn to wait patiently while listening to enthusiastic conversations about everything from last night's supper to a forthcoming wedding.'

'Not the weather?' Janie interrupted. 'That's our favourite topic of conversation.'

'They don't need to talk about the weather. The sun shines most days, spring arrives at the beginning of March, the days warm up and it's not until the end of October that it's cold enough for a coat. Although the Italians feel the slightest drop in temperature. It's quite funny to see them wrapped in their woollens in April. And then there's the rain. Great thundery showers that appear from nowhere and the electric storms. I could stand on the balcony, just off my bedroom and watch the sky light up. You could almost smell it when it was on its way. The air buzzed with it and the wind would drop. No rain, but explosions of light in great white sheets across the sky. It was like having a front row seat at the theatre with a performance of Verdi's *Rigoletto* playing out right in front of you. Then the lightning would pass and there would be a massive downpour for maybe half an hour. Afterwards everything smelled fresh and new. It was magical.'

'You had a balcony off your bedroom?' An image appeared in Janie's mind, of grand villas that until now she had only seen in magazines.

'I took a job with a family. Signor Dutti is a banker.'

'A wealthy banker, I'm guessing?' Phyllis asked.

'Most Italian bankers are wealthy,' Jessica replied, grinning.

'You enjoyed your time with the family?' Phyllis bent down to pick off a few deadheads from some winter pansies.

'I loved it. Signora Dutti was very easy going, as long as I kept the children clean and entertained. And then I made friends with Luigi and it turns out his father and the Duttis know each other. Oh, I don't know. To be honest, I'm just a simple girl who enjoys a simple life. I had no idea that befriending Luigi would bring so many complications with it.'

Phyllis put her hand on Jessica's arm. 'Sounds like your friend has a complicated past? May I make a suggestion?' Phyllis said, pinching out the new shoots from a honeysuckle that wound its way across the pergola.

'All suggestions gratefully received,' Janie said, smiling.

'You say Luigi has phoned his father,' Phyllis continued. 'When he arrives perhaps he will have some answers. He may know why this Bertie Williams came to Tamarisk Bay.'

Janie muttered something under her breath.

'What's that, dear?'

Janie didn't want to think about the bloodied shirt and the constant niggle at the back of her mind that Luigi had still not told her the whole truth. Perhaps Phyllis was right. Once Mr Denaro senior arrived things might start to become clearer.

'One thing's for sure,' Jessica chipped in, 'if we don't do something soon I have a dreadful feeling Luigi will be questioned again. DS Bright has a bee in his bonnet about something, he must have found evidence and decided that evidence points to a crime, with Luigi being his prime suspect.'

Chapter 17

Tuesday morning - Tidehaven Railway Station

It had been a busy Easter weekend for Robbie Golding. Plenty of day-trippers came to Tamarisk Bay and Tidehaven by coach, but there were plenty more who preferred the train, so the station taxi rank was a good place to pick up fares. This was Robbie's fourth year driving his taxi and he liked to have an imaginary bet with himself as to who might want a taxi ride. People arriving with luggage were a bit of a giveaway, but often family or friends would be there to meet them. Elderly folk with their walking sticks were his favourites. They were always ready to chat to him about anything and everything. Then there were the regulars whose favourite haunt was *The Dolphin*. It had gained quite a reputation, with Londoners saying they sold the best fish and chips for miles around.

It was still school holidays, but the Tuesday after the bank holiday was bound to be a bit quieter, giving him a chance to catch up on the crossword. He was just about halfway through it when the 10.05 from Charing Cross was due in. He put his pen down and watched the steady stream of passengers come out of the station.

The last person to emerge from the station forecourt was a tall, middle-aged gentleman, wearing a heavy overcoat and Trilby hat, carrying a small leather suitcase in one hand and a slim attaché case in the other.

'Need a lift, sir?' Robbie smiled at the visitor, whose expression was one of bewilderment. 'Down on holiday, are you?'

The visitor was silent, turning to put down his suitcase.

'Looking for a hotel, are we?' Robbie asked.

'*Si*, a hotel, *grazie.*' The man said.

'Ah, not speak the lingo, eh? No problemo. Let's take that case and we'll get you down to the Royal. That's it, in you get.' Robbie gestured to the man to get into the back of the taxi, while he put his case into the boot.

Ten minutes later he pulled up in front of the Royal Elizabeth Hotel.

'Here we are, sir,' he said, getting out of the cab and opening the door for his customer.

'*Quanto?* How much?' the Italian asked, his thick accent causing Robbie to frown. The frown soon disappeared when his customer thrust a note into his hand and waved at him to keep the change. 'Your card, please? If I need you again.'

'Ah, yes, of course.' Robbie handed over a little black and white card, pleased he had remembered to keep a few in the taxi. He was so rarely asked for one. Most of the locals knew the phone numbers of the taxi ranks by heart.

An hour later and Robbie pulled up again outside the hotel. He wasn't going to pass up such a good tipper. If he had to work a double shift, so be it.

'Where to this time, sir?' he asked.

The customer waved a piece of paper at him with a handwritten address.

'No problem, it's only a couple of minutes from here. You might like to walk it another time. The route is pretty straightforward.'

Robbie turned the car radio on and began humming to the Simon and Garfunkel track. If his customer didn't

148

want to talk, he would just have to listen to Robbie's choice of music, like it or not.

As he pulled up outside the Chandler house he noticed the sign on the door.

'Ah, it looks like Mr Chandler is closed for the Easter holiday. Were you hoping for an appointment with him? We're lucky to have him here in Tamarisk Bay. I'm not surprised his reputation has spread. I said to my Vi the other day, *Vi, we're lucky to have that Mr Chandler.*'

Robbie paused his story-telling when there was a knock on the window of the driver's door. The Italian was holding out a note, waiting to pay him.

'Oh no, sir, it's not that much. Like I say, it's a short journey. Wait while I get you some change.' He took the note and turned to get his money pouch from the glove compartment. When he looked up again his customer had walked up to the front door of the physiotherapy practice and was ringing the bell.

'I'll be off then,' Robbie muttered to himself.

As Philip Chandler opened the front door he heard the taxi pull away.

'Can I help you?' he said, holding Charlie's collar to stop him sniffing at the person who was standing on his doorstep.

'I am looking for my son, Luigi Denaro. I am Alberto Denaro. He told me this address.' The Italian spoke slowly, stumbling over each word. His English was good, but took a while to come readily to his mind. For these first few hours in England it was as though he had to rehearse each sentence in his mind before saying it aloud.

'Signor Denaro, do come in. Sorry, I didn't know you were coming. Does Luigi know you are here?'

The Italian followed Philip through the hallway and

into the sitting room.

'Do take a seat, can I offer you a drink? Coffee, tea?'

Alberto watched Philip as he navigated his way past the various pieces of furniture scattered around the room, the only indication of his blindness being the dog walking so closely beside him.

'Nothing, thank you. Is my son here?'

'No. He is staying at a nearby guest house. I will phone him for you. I'm sure he will be delighted to know you are here.'

'No, he will not.' Alberto chose a seat to one side of the fireplace and watched as Philip sat opposite him, with the dog laying down at his feet, his head resting on Philip's feet. 'I would be grateful if you could telephone.'

Philip stood, signalling to Charlie that they were moving out into the hallway. He stood at the hall table and dialled the number for the *Summer Guest House*. Rosetta picked up the phone at the first ring. 'I have not seen Luigi this morning, but I will put a note in his room,' she told Philip.

Returning to the sitting room, Philip explained, 'It seems we may have a little wait before Luigi arrives. Are you sure you won't have a drink? Why don't you come through to the kitchen, we can chat while we wait for the kettle to boil?'

Perhaps it was the language barrier, or a barrier of another kind, preventing an easy conversation between the two men. Regardless of the reason, Philip was relieved when the doorbell rang to signify Luigi's arrival. He let him in, asking him to follow him through to the kitchen.

Without sight Philip had learned to use his hearing to great effect. It was easy enough to tell where someone was standing when they spoke, but on this occasion it was the silence between father and son that told him so much more.

'Why don't you both go into the sitting room? It will be more comfortable for you to chat. I've got a few things to sort out in my treatment room, if you'll excuse me?'

Whether they were grateful for his withdrawal was impossible to know, as neither replied. Charlie followed Philip through to the clinic, where in truth he had nothing to tidy, but was relieved to be away from the tension emanating between the two Italians.

'Your friend dies and you come. Shame you couldn't show the same level of concern over your own wife.' Luigi spat his words out, avoiding his father's gaze.

'I don't know what you want me to say.'

'You ruined my mother's life and now you've ruined mine. If you hadn't sent Bertie to come after me he wouldn't be dead and I wouldn't be under suspicion.'

'Why are you under suspicion?'

'The police, they think I did something. They've questioned me twice now and they are keeping my passport. Scared I'll run.' Luigi glared at his father, taking a deep breath before continuing. 'You thought I'd taken something from your study, something that could get you into trouble, so you sent Bertie to follow me to get it back. You couldn't even do your own dirty work.'

'Luigi, you're not thinking straight.'

'You knew it was me. The night that *mamma* died. You thought I'd expose your dirty secrets.'

'I don't have any dirty secrets as you put it. Yes, I knew you'd been through my study - I know it could only have been you. But I have nothing to hide. Whatever

151

you think you found, it isn't important.'

Luigi scrunched up his fists so tight that his knuckles were white. 'You twist everything to suit yourself, you always have.'

'You hate me that much?' Alberto moved towards the fireplace, picking up one of the ornaments from the mantelpiece. It was made of glass, a winter's scene that became a snowy one as he shook it.

'She killed herself because of what you did. Hate you? Yes, I hate you.' Luigi shouted, while his father still had his back turned towards him.

'I loved your mother. I'm just sorry I couldn't make her happy.' Alberto spoke as though he was talking to himself, arguing with his own memories.

For a few moments there was silence while each man was absorbed in his own thoughts.

'You were the one to find her,' Alberto continued. 'That image must haunt you.'

He turned back to face his son, but Luigi was careful to avoid his gaze.

'I was convinced you were having an affair, that's why I broke into your study.' Luigi's tone was full of spite and anger.

'There was no affair. Your mother and I had good times when we were first married.'

'And what? When I was born I ruined everything? So now I'm to blame for her misery? For the failure of your marriage?' Luigi thumped his fists on the arm of the settee, making it shake.

'No, *figlio mio*. You are not to blame for any of it. It's not your fault your mother died and it's not your fault that Bertie died.' Alberto stopped speaking and waited for his words to sink in. 'I know you didn't kill him, I know my son is not a murderer.'

'You didn't send Bertie here to England?' For the first time in their conversation Luigi held his father's gaze.

Alberto sat and reached his hand across the table towards his son. 'No,' he said, his expression confirming his reply.

'Why did he come then? How did he know I was here in Tamarisk Bay?'

'I genuinely don't know. He must have had his own reasons for coming here. Let's walk together and talk some more. Mr Chandler has accommodated us for long enough.'

'I have nothing to say to you.'

Philip had the radio on, letting his favourite classical music station relax him. The volume was turned low, so when he heard a door slam it made him jump, and Charlie bark.

'Shush, Charlie. Come on, let's see what's going on, shall we?'

Returning to the sitting room Philip heard footsteps pacing across the carpet. 'Is everything alright? I heard a door, I thought perhaps I had another visitor?' He smiled, hoping to keep the tone of his voice as light-hearted as possible.

It was Signor Denaro senior who replied. 'My son has gone. I am sorry we have troubled you.'

'I'm guessing Luigi has gone back to the guest house.'

'Yes, Signor Chandler, my son is very angry with me.' He was standing by the fireplace, looking at the photo frames lined up along the mantelpiece. One of the photos were of Greg and Janie on their wedding day. He picked it up, running his finger absent-mindedly over the frame, before replacing it carefully in exactly the same position as before.

'Angry that you are here in England?'

'In England, in Italy, it is all the same.' His voice carried a despondency that Philip would have seen reflected in his face, if was able.

'I'm happy to speak to him if you think it will help.'

Only Charlie watched Alberto as he moved to the door. 'Thank you again for your hospitality. I must go now.'

'Do you have somewhere to stay?'

'I am at the Royal Elizabeth Hotel. I have to attend to arrangements for a business associate. I will be there for a few days. It was a pleasure to meet you, Signor Chandler. *Arrivederci*.'

Chapter 18

Tuesday afternoon - the Chandler household

A little later that day, Jessica and Janie left Phyllis' cottage and returned to Philip's house.

'Michelle is missing her grandad,' Janie said, settling her daughter into Philip's arms. 'We've been introducing Jessica to *Jefferson's* and she seems to have scored quite a hit with Richie,' Janie said, grinning. 'Then we dropped round to see Phyllis.'

'How is she?' Philip said, jiggling the baby around a little, and being rewarded with a gurgle.

'She's amazing is what she is,' Jessica replied. 'Ten years on and she's barely aged. The woman is an inspiration. What about your day?'

'It's been interesting.'

'What have we missed?' Janie opened the fridge and took out a few dishes of leftovers from the previous night's supper.

'Luigi's father is here. He's booked into the Royal Elizabeth.'

'He came quickly then. Did you get a sense of their conversation?'

Philip shook his head. 'They had a row and Luigi stormed off. It can't be easy for Mr Denaro.'

'I'd be pretty angry too if my father made my mother so miserable she ended up killing herself.'

'There are two sides to every story,' Jessica said. 'I'd like to meet this Signor Denaro for myself, see if I can unravel some of the mysteries concerning the Denaro family.'

'I'm not sure we should get involved.' Philip rocked Michelle to and fro as she started to cry.

'We're already involved, dad. Jessica is right. Let's grab a quick sandwich, then we can take a walk down to the hotel, introduce ourselves and offer to take him on a little tour of Tamarisk Bay. There's no harm in being friendly, is there?'

Drawing a blank at the hotel, Jessica and Janie pushed the pram over to the *Summer Guest House*. Rosetta confirmed that Luigi had stormed in late morning and gone straight to his room.

'Is it okay if we go up?' Janie asked, taking Michelle out of the pram.

'Leave the baby with me,' Rosetta said. 'She is a good excuse for me to sit for a while and rest.'

Janie knocked gently on the bedroom door and when there was no response she knocked again a little louder.

'Go away,' Luigi's voice sounded muffled.

'We're coming in,' Jessica said, easing the door open to find Luigi laying on the bed, with his back to them. She pulled a chair over from one side of the room and gestured for Janie to sit down. 'What's going on, Luigi? Philip says your father is here. We walked over to the hotel to meet him, but he was out. Have you two had a row?'

'All we do is row,' Luigi swung his legs off the bed and sat up. His face was damp, his hair dishevelled.

'You asked him to come and he came,' Janie said. 'You should be pleased.'

'He has come for Bertie, not for me.'

A few moments passed when no-one spoke. Then Janie said, 'Does Bertie have family in Italy?'

Luigi stood, pulled the bedspread up to cover the bed and smoothed out the wrinkles in it. Then he sat on the edge of the bed again.

'In England?' Jessica asked.

'I think he has a sister. She lives in the north of England somewhere. I know very little about him. Like I said, he was a business associate of my father.'

Jessica stood at the bedroom window, looking out over the back garden.

'Luigi,' Jessica moved towards him, blocking out the light from the window, forcing him to focus on her. 'We are your friends, but whatever you have done you will only make things worse by lying.'

'You say you are my friend, and you call me a liar.' He jumped up from the bed and put his face close to Jessica's. 'You know nothing about me. I have done nothing wrong.'

'So prove it,' Janie said, moving over to stand beside Jessica. 'Tell us what happened the night Bertie died.'

He pushed past them, without replying. Leaving them both with no more to say until Michelle's hunger cries broke the silence.

A few moments later Janie and Jessica returned to the sitting room where Rosetta was chanting something in Italian to Michelle, who seemed contented to listen.

'What's she saying?' Janie whispered as they approached.

'Maybe she's praying. It sounds like the Hail Mary.'

Rosetta fell silent as they approached, passing Michelle to her mother.

'Was that a lullaby you were singing to her?' Janie said.

'A song my mother used to sing to me. She had a beautiful singing voice. My father too. Sometimes in the evening after supper, he would sing pieces from *La Boheme* to us. But my voice is like a frog. Isn't it Michelle, your *Zia* Rosetta does not sing, she croaks.'

Michelle gave a little gurgle in response.

'I don't think she agrees with you,' Janie said, laughing.

Rosetta handed Michelle back to Janie, then held her arms out as if she was grateful she no longer had the responsibility of caring. Her expression was stern. 'I had two guests, Luigi and Mr Williams,' she said, shaking her head. 'Now one is dead and the other, well, I would prefer if he found another place to stay.' Her voice rose to a shrill pitch, disturbing Michelle, who now started to cry.

Janie and Jessica exchanged glances.

'You want him to move out?' Janie said.

'Yes, it is best. He is not happy. I am not happy. I would like the place to myself. You understand?'

'Do you want me to tell him?' Janie said.

'Yes please. I am sorry, but I want to be on my own.'

Janie and Jessica talked through the conversation on the way back to Philip's house.

'To be honest, I feel bad that we didn't get Luigi to move out before now,' Janie said. 'We still have our doubts about him and yet we've left him with Rosetta, it's not fair on her.'

'What do you suggest we do now then? He'll feel like a parcel being shoved around. Although really he's brought some of it on himself by not being straight with us.'

'If he moves back in with you and dad, at least you'll be there to keep an eye on him. We can hardly expect him to stay at the Royal Elizabeth, with his dad along the corridor. Anyway, I've been thinking,' Janie said, continuing an internal conversation she was having with herself, 'now the Easter weekend is over the police must have the results of the post mortem.'

'I doubt the police will share them with you. They'll only want to tell the next of kin.'

'But if there is no next of kin, then what? How about I go with Signor Denaro to the police station?'

Jessica bent down towards the pram. 'Michelle, your mother is a force to be reckoned with. You'd better grow up quickly to keep an eye on her.'

'I'm only trying to be helpful.'

'Ah, in that case...I'm guessing Greg has given up trying to rein in his wife's enthusiasm for amateur sleuthing?'

'Like I said, I'm just trying to be helpful,' Janie said, grinning.

Having left Michelle with Jessica and Philip, Janie caught up with Alberto Denaro on his return to the hotel. He'd had a short walk along the seafront, trying to work out the best way to prove to his son that he was on his side.

When he walked into the hotel reception Janie recognised his him as Luigi's father straightaway. He had the same sculptured features, the deep forehead and, despite the flickers of silver running through his hair, it was easy to see why Eloise would have fallen for him all those years ago.

Janie introduced herself and shook Alberto's hand.

'Will you help me?' he said and she was taken back to the moment when Hugh Furness asked her the same thing, all those months ago, before Michelle was born.

'Let's go to the police station together,' she said by way

of reply.

Alberto Denaro decided he would approach this meeting like any other. The police had information that he needed. His son was a suspect and yet there was no crime. If he was back at home, in Italy, he would make a couple of phone calls and the matter would be resolved. Luigi's passport would be returned to him and he would be free to leave. More than that, there would be an apology.

These are the things he expected when he walked into the interview room and sat beside Janie. Detective Sergeant Bright sat opposite them, his pencil poised, a packet of cigarettes to one side of his notebook, an overflowing ashtray on the other.

But when Alberto and Janie emerged into bright sunlight about half an hour later, nothing had been resolved. Instead, Alberto had been subjected to a barrage of questions about his association with Bertie Williams and his son's involvement in his business affairs. There was a moment when Alberto could no longer contain his temper. DS Bright had asked about Luigi's missing briefcase. Alberto was certain the detective had insinuated that his son had fabricated the existence of the briefcase.

'You are calling my son a liar. I won't listen to any more,' he said, his voice suddenly booming around the little interview room. It was only when Janie put her hand on his shoulder that he was able to regain control.

At the end of the interview Janie asked for news of the post-mortem.

'Mr Denaro would like to know the cause of Mr Williams' death. They were friends for many years. He has a right to know.'

'Mr Denaro has no rights in this matter. Neither do you, Mrs Juke. However, I can tell you that the initial post-mortem was inconclusive. I have requested another.'

'Inconclusive. What does that mean?'

'Exactly what it says. At present we can't be certain as to the cause of death. Until we have more information I am keeping an open mind.'

'So my son is still a suspect?' Alberto said.

'My advice to you, sir, is to recommend to your son that he tells us the whole truth about his movements on Friday evening.'

'He has done nothing wrong.'

'Then he has nothing to fear.'

'Thank you for coming with me today.' Alberto held his hand out. With a brief nod and a handshake, he turned and walked down towards the promenade to return to the hotel. In the twenty-minute walk back to her dad's house Janie had time to mull over events so far.

DS Bright clearly had reason to suspect Luigi. Did he just suspect him of lying, or of something far worse? The blood on Luigi's shirt still worried her. Her instincts told her there was a simple explanation for it, but if she shared the discovery with the police it could land Luigi in even more trouble. It was a difficult line to tread between protecting her aunt's friend and withholding potential evidence. *It's only evidence if there's been a crime.* She needed to sit tight until the results of the second post-mortem were through. If the police were going to make a move, perhaps even arrest Luigi, they would only do so once they knew for sure that Bertie Williams had been murdered.

Chapter 19

Wednesday - the Chandler household

Philip laid back in his favourite armchair and positioned his feet so that Charlie could lay his head across them. *Desert Island Discs* was on the radio and as one of his favourite Frank Sinatra records came on he tapped his fingers on the arm of the chair in time with the beat.

There were no appointments today. He'd decided to close the practice for a few extra days following the Easter holiday to spend more time with Jessica. But now she was back, it seemed that trouble had followed her.

Their early childhood years had been carefree. He remembered spending hours kicking a football around, with little Jess struggling to keep up with him. Whatever Philip tried, his little sister attempted to copy. But with five years between them he would often get into trouble for getting her into scrapes. Like the time he climbed the neighbour's apple tree, only to find Jess struggling up behind him before he could stop her. He still remembered the dread in his stomach as he watched her fall from one of the lowest branches, with a scream that brought his mother running out in her apron, thinking that someone had died.

When Philip had enlisted in the army, Jessica was still too young to work, even as a volunteer. And, thankfully, by the time she was old enough, the war was over.

After much badgering from Philip, Jessica was persuaded to take a college secretarial course. But even Philip admitted that was a mistake. She was far too fidgety to do office work and too independent to make a good secretary. Their parents laughed when Jess recounted an exchange she had had in her one and only interview for a copy typist.

'I imagine it will suit me very well,' she had said towards the end of the interview, to which the response from the interviewer was, 'you will do well to leave your imagination at home, Miss Chandler. There's no time for dreaming in this job.'

Needless to say, she was unsuccessful.

Philip's attention was brought back to the present when Charlie lifted his head away from Philip's feet. Even without that movement Philip's senses were so finely tuned he quickly detected when someone came into the room.

'Jess, come and sit with me, let's chat. Turn the radio down if you like.'

Jessica plumped up the cushions in one of the armchairs, settling herself down opposite Philip.

'Bit of a whirlwind few days for you. Not the best homecoming,' Philip said, holding his hand out towards his sister.

'I was looking forward to showing Luigi around my old haunts, thought it would give me a chance for a spot of reminiscing. But now, with what's happened, well I don't much feel like spending any time with him to be honest.'

'He's a troubled soul, but he's had a lot to cope with. Janie told me about his mother. And to be the person who found her - I'm not sure how you would recover from something like that.'

Jessica took her brother's hand in hers and squeezed it. 'I've been so lucky, Phil. I've had a ball these last nine years.'

'All those years you were stuck looking after us, you deserved your years of freedom. You gave up a lot for us, Jess.'

'I didn't give up a single thing. I had a great time when I lived with you two. Don't you remember, all those summers I spent at the Bathing Pool. Janie was at school and you were doing your physio training and I was lazing around, sunning myself in-between practising my dives from the top board.'

'You've always loved a challenge.'

'I've met some lovely people on my travels, adventurers like me. Looking for the simple life. I moved around, slept on friends' sofas, on beaches, even on someone's floor one time. I barely needed any money, food was so cheap, all I needed was enough for my bus or train ticket to the next place, so I just picked up work when I needed to. Shop work, waitressing, I helped a friend sell sandwiches on a beach in Spain. Then I travelled around Italy for a while, and when I was in Rome I struck lucky. I heard about a family who needed a nanny. They wanted someone to help out with the children, with a bit of housework thrown in.'

'Sounds perfect,' Philip said.

'Yes. A lovely family. I lived in, even had the use of their car. The Dutti family have a beautiful apartment in the centre of Rome and a villa in Anzio; you were there in the war, weren't you? Although I doubt you'd recognise it now; it's so pretty, fountains and piazzas, sandy beaches, fish restaurants.'

'You're right. Not the Anzio I remember,' Philip said, 'and thank goodness for it.'

'Being so close to Rome it's perfect for Italian families who want to have a seaside place for the long summer holidays. Often the mother takes them to the coast for the whole two months and the father joins them at weekends. Signor Dutti is a banker.'

'And you met Luigi at the Dutti's villa?'

Jessica tutted by way of a reply and then she said, 'I met Luigi by chance. I was with the family at their Anzio villa. The children are both learning to play the piano, so I used to drop them off at the piano teacher's house every Thursday and I'd have an hour or so to myself. I'd walk to the end of the harbour and watch the fishermen mending their nets. Then I'd grab a cappuccino in my favourite bar and people watch. The elegance of the Italian people fascinates me. They can make the most basic of outfits look like they just stepped off a catwalk.'

'And Luigi was a passer-by?'

'No, he was helping to run the bar. Mario, the owner, is a good friend of his. You have to understand that in Italy it is all about who you know, not what you know.'

'We might call it nepotism over here.'

'But it's a way of life for them. Family is everything. Anyway, I heard Luigi speaking English to some of the customers and I was astonished at his accent, or rather lack of it. So, I got chatting to him and we hit it off. When he found out where I'd lived and grew up he was fascinated. He'd heard a lot about England, of course, from his mother, but they never visited. I must admit, I thought that a bit strange.'

'Why come to England when you've got the whole of Italy to explore. I guess a lot of southern Europeans end up staying in their own country for their whole lives. It's only us from the frozen north who are tempted south by all that sunshine.'

They both laughed for a moment and then Jessica continued.

'I know what you mean. Anyway, I often ran into Luigi when I visited Mario's and we would chat. I suppose outsiders would see our friendship as unusual, but there's something about him, a vulnerability. Sometimes he'd join me on my walk along the harbour. He was forever asking me questions about England. Then not long after I met him the Dutti family threw a big party for their silver wedding anniversary, to which I was invited.'

'Did you invite Luigi?' Janie asked.

Jessica shifted her feet a little whilst trying not to disturb Charlie. 'No, but he was there. We got chatting and it turns out he's known the family for years. Apparently, his father and Signor Dutti are business associates.'

'Seems like most of Italy were business associates of Mr Denaro. And you met Luigi's father at the party?'

'No, I get the feeling parties aren't really Mr Denaro's thing. I'm not too sure why Luigi was there to be honest with you. He didn't really chat to anyone except me, he spent most of the time sitting outside on the veranda, as far away from the general festivities as possible. Then a couple of weeks after the party Signora Dutti called me into the sitting room. The children were outside playing. She said she was very sorry, but she had to let me go.'

'That's strange she didn't give you a reason.'

'She just said they wouldn't be needing me anymore. She asked me to leave within two weeks. It was so difficult telling the children, I didn't know what to say to them. She gave me a month's money and wished me well, but it broke my heart. Ricardo and Flavia were such sweet children. Their little faces when I told them, the whole thing haunted me for weeks.'

'Maybe money was tight for the family and they needed to make savings.'

'Signor Dutti is an Italian banker. Forget all you know about English bank managers, this is another league entirely. Trust me, this was not about a shortage of money. I've wracked my brains but I don't understand what it was all about.'

'Anyway, when I told Luigi he sympathised, but he said the Duttis were typical business people and nothing they did would surprise him. He was quite scathing, actually.'

They moved through to the kitchen and while Jessica prepared some sandwiches she told Philip the rest of the story. She explained how she'd worked briefly in Rome as a chambermaid, keeping in occasional contact with Luigi. Philip said very little, nodding occasionally and purposely dropping some cheese on the floor for Charlie to hoover up.

'That must have left you pretty disenchanted with Italy?' Philip asked.

'It was just one family. One bad experience. Like I said, I've been lucky. There was a time when I thought I would spend the rest of my life in Italy. The people are so warm and hospitable. They welcome you into their homes, their hearts. I love everything about the life there.' Jessica got up, patting Charlie by way of an apology for disturbing him. 'When Luigi found out I was heading home he asked if he could come with me. I'll admit I didn't think the adventure would turn out quite the way it has.'

Jessica flicked her hair back from her face, looking at

her brother as though searching his face for answers. 'I used to believe I was good at summing people up. But Luigi has me stumped. When I arrived I told Janie there were no mysteries to unravel. Maybe I was wrong.'

Jessica pulled out a makeup bag from her shoulder bag, taking out a bottle of nail varnish and setting it down on the kitchen table. 'In case you wonder what I'm up to, I'm going to paint my nails. I keep meaning to tell Janie how impressed I am with the state of her manicure. I thought she would be a nail biter forever.'

'Ah, she has Libby to thank for that.'

'Phyllis's granddaughter? She's a reporter, isn't she?'

Philip smiled. 'Bit of a live wire, but good fun. She's ambitious, so I wouldn't be surprised if we see her by-line on a Fleet Street rag one of these days.'

'Phil, I've been thinking. When things have settled a bit how about you and I check out some old haunts, see what's changed. Maybe the odd day trip?'

Philip bent down and massaged behind one of Charlie's ears, sending the dog into paroxysms of delight. 'You hear that Charlie, looks like we've got to prepare ourselves for a challenge.'

'When was the last time you caught a train? How about a day in Brighton, we could sit on the seafront, eat fish and chips.' There was a bright confidence in her tone, which made Philip smile.

'Your niece is more like you than you could ever imagine. She doesn't see barriers either. Everything is possible in Janie's eyes, it's just that some things take a little longer to work out.'

'Exactly. So, train to Brighton, Charlie? What do you think? Can you and I keep your master out of mischief for the day?'

By way of a reply Charlie repositioned himself so that his body was laying on Philip's feet and his head was resting against Jessica's leg.

'I think that's a yes, then,' Jessica said.

Chapter 20

Wednesday - the Summer Guest House

Alberto Denaro removed the pocket-sized diary from his briefcase and flicked through the pages. He had had to cancel two meetings already and it was doubtful he would be back in time for the next one, which was scheduled for three days' time.

In many ways it had been a wasted journey. He had come because he hoped his son was finally asking for his help. Instead, he would barely talk to him. There was Bertie's funeral to organise, but everything in England took so long, and the police were sniffing around, which was delaying matters even more.

It was ridiculous that his son should be under suspicion. Luigi didn't have it in him to kill anyone. He was too much like his mother. Their nature was sullen, with all their emotions on the outside, but without any inner core of strength. It was all such a waste.

Eloise had never trusted him to make her happy. No matter what gifts he bought her, fur coats, jewellery, perfume; she would smile briefly, thank him, then a day or so later she would sink back into her gloom. His business gave him the excuse to be away from home as much as possible and so they lived a life more apart than together. But, with Luigi spending so much time with his mother, it was inevitable he would turn out like her.

Alberto's dreams of one day handing over his business to his son were just that, dreams. Luigi preferred to work in a bar, rather than learn how to conduct successful business transactions. Everyone in the business world knew the name of Alberto Denaro and that made him proud. There was so much he could have taught his son. So much money to be made.

Alberto went into the little bathroom attached to his hotel bedroom. He switched on the light over the mirror and stared at his reflection. The bare bulb cast a yellowy glow over his face, making his skin look sallow, making him feel tired. He ran his fingers through his hair, noticing the peppering of grey across his fringe and in his sideboards. His wife had loved his jet-black hair. The first time they met she teased him, saying she was convinced he was a film star. '*Are you sure you aren't Robert Taylor in disguise?*' she would say, laughing.

'Oh, Eloise,' he whispered to his reflection. 'If it hadn't been for the war, maybe we would have been happy.'

He ran cold water into the basin and splashed his face, grabbing one of the hand towels on his way back into the bedroom.

'*Basta, enough,*' he thought as he took his jacket from the back of the chair and smoothed out the creases in it.

It was a pleasant day for a walk. The usual drab grey skies that England was famous for had held off since his arrival. Nevertheless, he took an umbrella with him in one hand and his attaché case in the other. The hotel receptionist had made a great fuss of giving him a local street map and drawing the route to the guest house for him. But it was simple, just a short walk along the seafront. As he ambled, he looked down onto the shingle beach, surprised to see so many families seemingly enjoying what was to him a chilly afternoon. He wore his overcoat, while they wore bathing costumes.

One family had a blanket spread out on the pebbles, with a great spread of food; sandwiches, cakes, biscuits. He watched as the little boy, who couldn't have been much more than five or six picked up each sandwich, took a bite from it, then put it back down on the blanket. His father started shouting at him, the child started to cry, until the boy's mother pulled him towards her and gave him a hug. She patted the space beside her, opened a packet of biscuits and gave the child one. The father got up and walked down to the water's edge, throwing pebbles into the water, watching them as they skimmed along the surface, before dropping down into the murky sea.

When Alberto reached the guest house he hesitated a moment before pressing the bell. It seemed that as soon as the bell rang Rosetta opened the door, almost as if she had been anticipating his arrival.

'Yes?' she said, holding the door open, but standing in the doorway.

'I am Alberto Denaro. My son has been staying with you.' He stood on the doorstep and waited. It was strange speaking in English when they were both Italian, but somehow it seemed like the right thing to do.

'Ah, yes, Luigi's father. *Piacere*. It is nice to meet you. He is not here.' Her discomfort at the thought of inviting him inside was undisguised. The Denaro family and its associates had brought her nothing but bad luck.

'May I come in?' He waited, wondering if she would relent or if he would have to return on another occasion. Perhaps he could accompany his son, although that would bring a whole other range of difficulties.

'Your son is not here,' she repeated.

'No, but my associate, Mr Williams. I have come to

settle his affairs.' He wondered if it might help his cause to put things onto a more official footing. 'There is paperwork to complete, you understand?'

'Ah, yes. Please come in.'

She stepped back and gestured for him to enter. They stood awkwardly, side by side in the hallway.

'The police took his passport,' she said, wondering what paperwork might be needed to organise a funeral.

'May I see his room?' At last he came to the reason for his visit.

Rosetta hesitated, trying to determine what it was about this man that made her uncomfortable.

'Why do you want to see his room?'

'As I said, I have to arrange his funeral. I imagine his clothes are still here?'

'Ah, yes.' A picture formed in her mind of the day she had to choose clothes to dress her husband's body. She put her hands up to her face, closing her eyes for a moment, hoping to dispel the image. Then she gestured to Alberto, leading him up to the second floor and pointing to the door of Room 3. 'You go in. I do not like to. Not since...'

'I understand. It must have been a shock for you.' He pushed open the bedroom door, standing for a moment with his hand on the door handle, waiting for Rosetta to move away.

'I will be in the kitchen,' she said, turning to retreat down the staircase, away from the grim reminders of death.

Once inside the room Alberto stood at the doorway and looked around. He flicked the light switch on to bring brightness to the otherwise gloomy surroundings, made even more gloomy by the heavy satin curtains that were still drawn closed.

Once in the bedroom he began working his way through the tallboy, running his fingers around the sides and back of each drawer. He didn't know what he was looking for. All he knew for certain was that there had to be a reason for Bertie's visit to Tamarisk Bay. If he could discover that reason, perhaps it would explain all the events that had happened since then.

As he worked his way around the room, he thought of Bertie's friendship. They had both seen their businesses grow and become increasingly successful. There had been times when Alberto envied his friend a little. Bertie had no distractions, no wife, no children. He was able to focus wholeheartedly on his work, without the guilt Alberto seemed to carry with him, like a permanent sack on his back. When Alberto had opened Luigi's letter and discovered his son had gone to England, Bertie was the first person he told.

'I have let my son down,' he told him. 'I should have been the one to take him to England, to visit his mother's birthplace. Making the journey together might have helped to heal the rift that has always been between us.'

Alberto returned to his search, trying to rid his mind of painful memories. Having been through each of the drawers and found nothing, he stood for a moment and looked at the bed. The impressions on the pillow and blankets still held the shape of his friend's body. It was as though his spirit was still there resting.

He walked to the window, pulled back the curtains and looked out over the back garden. The grass was a vivid green. He smiled for a moment, remembering how much his wife missed the English lawns. There was nowhere for grass amongst their verandas and patios at the seaside villa. Perhaps he should have dug up some of the paving. Maybe it would have given her pleasure.

He moved about the room quietly, trying to cause the minimum disruption. Moving over to the walnut wardrobe he tugged at the double doors. The wood was slightly warped, making one of the doors stick on its bottom edge. He tugged again and the doors flew open, revealing just three hangers, carrying two suits and a casual jacket. Bertie had clearly not intended staying for long.

He searched each of the pockets in the jacket, hesitating for a moment when he thought he heard footsteps outside the door. He held his breath, listening, looking at the door handle, wondering if it would turn and someone would enter. He would be made to look like a thief, needing to find an excuse for rifling through his friend's belongings. When there was no further sound or movement he continued, sliding his hand into a small pocket, fashioned from the silk lining of the jacket. He pulled out an envelope. He took his spectacles out of his jacket pocket and put them on. But, in truth, he didn't need the spectacles to recognise the handwriting. A single word was written on the envelope. The word was 'Bertie'.

Turning the envelope over he ran his finger across the torn flap. It was as though the recipient had ripped it open, desperate to read its contents. Alberto eased the envelope open with great care, sliding his hand inside and pulling out a single sheet of ivory writing paper. It had been folded twice and was blank on one side, so it wasn't until he opened it fully that he could confirm the writing on the letter matched that on the envelope. The handwriting was his wife's, his Eloise.

He closed his eyes for a moment, dreading what he was about to read. Then he opened them again and read the words.

Dearest Bertie

I ask for forgiveness from you, from my son and even from Alberto. My love for you has sustained me for many years, but it has also diminished me, as a mother and as a wife.

You are right that our love affair should never have been and yet I can't imagine a life without you in it. Please don't think badly of me. I can't wait to watch you fade. So, I take my leave of you my love and hope, with every fibre of my being, that we will meet again one day, in the piazza, by the fountain.

Yours, Eloise

As he reached the end of the letter Alberto dropped to the floor and knelt, holding the sheet of writing paper in his hands. 'Oh, Eloise, my sweet girl,' he said aloud to the empty room. The weight of his grief bore down on him as he bowed his head to his knees and cried.

It was an hour or so later before Alberto arrived at Philip's house. During that hour he had rehearsed a hundred different ways to tell his son the hardest news of all. That it was his mother who had been having an affair and that, ultimately, it was the dread of losing Bertie that had caused her to take her own life.

He still hadn't found the right words when he knocked on Philip's front door, half hoping to be told that his son was out. Instead, it was Luigi who answered the door. He glared at his father, holding the door partly open so that Alberto, once again, was left standing on the doorstep.

'Can I come in?' his voice was shaky, his mind in turmoil.

Luigi tutted and stood back. 'Do what you want. You usually do.'

Alberto moved forwards into the hallway, wondering how to make the next move. 'Is Mr Chandler at home?'

'Is it him you've come to see?'

'No, *figlio*, it's you. I need to talk with you.'

Luigi screwed his face up as though the thought of a conversation with his father was as distasteful as biting into a sour lemon.

'He's in the sitting room with Janie and Jessica. Probably talking about me and the trouble I've caused.'

'Oh, Luigi,' Alberto said, sighing in desperation.

'You'd better come through to the kitchen. We can talk there undisturbed.'

He gestured to his father to follow him through to the kitchen, then kept his back to him while he filled the kettle and put it on the gas.

'Luigi, don't bother with that just now. I'd rather you sat down. I need to explain something to you, it's difficult...'

Luigi paused for a moment before turning off the gas, but he remained standing, looking away from his father.

'If you won't look at me, I hope at least you will listen. I've been back to the guest house and I've been in Bertie's room.'

'Looking for more evidence against me? Even my own father thinks I'm guilty.'

'No, quite the opposite. I have been to Bertie's room to find something that would prove your innocence.'

Luigi turned around to face his father, his eyes narrowed, his forehead creased.

Alberto moved towards his son. Luigi didn't back away, but there was still distance between the two of them. A physical distance reinforcing the emotional chasm.

'Let me speak first. I need to tell you something.' Luigi said, taking a deep breath before continuing. 'I did go into Bertie's room that night. And the police know that. I haven't told them, but they know, I'm sure of it.'

Alberto sighed. This latest twist in events was like an unwanted guest at a party - unexpected and difficult to get rid of. 'Why did you lie?'

'Why do you think? I went into his room that evening. The next thing he's dead. I was the last person to see him alive.'

Luigi got up and moved to the door, leaving his father still trying to absorb his admission.

'Tell me exactly what happened, what you spoke about?'

'Go back to Italy, papà. Go back to your business meetings, your wheeling and dealing and leave me to meet my fate. If they want to arrest me, let them. I don't care anymore.'

Philip heard the front door bang and guessed whoever had left the house was not in the best of tempers. He nudged Charlie into action and followed him towards the kitchen. Not wanting to barge in, he knocked on the door before entering.

'Is everything alright?' Philip said, not knowing who he might be talking to. Then, hearing Alberto's voice he pushed the door open and waited.

'I am so sorry, Mr Chandler. You must think my son is very rude, slamming the door like that. He is very upset.'

'You have no need to apologise. He's been through a lot, it's understandable that he's upset.'

Philip eased a chair away from the table and sat, stretching his hand out to pat Charlie as he pushed up against his leg.

'My son blames me for all that is wrong in his life. Perhaps he is right. Perhaps if I'd spent less time trying to make money...' Alberto paused. 'May I pour myself a glass of water?'

'Of course, there is ice in the little top box of the fridge.'

Alberto ran the cold tap, filling one of the glasses that sat on the drainer. He took a few sips and then poured the remainder into the sink. 'But we cannot undo the past,' he said.

'No, you can't change what has gone. I know all about that.' Philip gave a wry smile.

'Of course, you have had to deal with great difficulties in your life. Losing your sight, trying to raise your daughter alone.'

'I wasn't alone. My sister was a wonderful support to us.' Philip paused, listening for any sound or movement to try to establish whether Alberto was sitting or standing. 'What can we do to help?'

'Do you think my son will be arrested?'

'The police want answers and at the moment they think Luigi is the only one who can provide them. Mr Denaro, do you know what your friend was doing here in Tamarisk Bay?'

'That's what my son asked me. And today I have found something that I think explains his visit.'

The conversation stopped briefly as Janie joined them.

She took some glasses from one of the cupboards, made a jug of orange squash and set it down on the table, pouring out a little for each of them. For a few moments they focused on their drinks. Then Janie said, 'Mr Denaro, can we rewind a moment? Can you tell me a little more about your relationship with Mr Williams? Was it purely a business association?'

Alberto stood and walked over towards Charlie, bending to stroke the dog's head. 'He is a very good dog, a good friend too?'

'I couldn't manage without him,' Philip said, laying his hand on Charlie's back and stroking him.

'Bertie was also a good friend. I met him many years ago, not long after the war had ended. I was building up my business and he was developing his. We had many of the same business associates, we would often bump into each other at meetings.' Alberto paused, replaying the memories of those times, memories that were now tainted by the letter in his pocket. 'Mr Chandler, you have lost your sight, but you have your family around you. I have the benefit of all my senses and yet I have been blind to many things.'

Janie reached her hand out towards Philip before saying, 'What was it you found, Mr Denaro?' She watched the Italian bow his head and waited for him to speak.

'I found this,' he said, taking the envelope from his pocket and handing it to Janie.

She held it in her hand for a moment, waiting for confirmation from him that she should open it.

'Read it please. But I cannot stay here to hear the words.'

This time the front door closed with barely a sound as Alberto Denaro stepped out into the quiet street.

Chapter 21

Wednesday afternoon - the Chandler household

It was mid-afternoon before Luigi returned to Philip's house. Michelle had been fed and changed and was now laying happily on Philip's lap. The radio was on and the background music gave an apparent peacefulness to the scene, while Janie's thoughts were anything but. Eloise's letter changed everything and now she had to find a way to tell Luigi the news she was certain would break his heart.

After Jessica had read the letter she said her overriding emotion was guilt.

'What do you have to feel guilty about?' Janie asked her aunt.

'I should have realised, asked more questions.'

'I'm sure that Luigi never guessed the truth, so your questions would have been pointless. It's a sad, sad story and the only people who know the truth of it are dead. Take yourself out and try not to think any more about it.'

'I'll go to the penny arcade on Tidehaven Pier. Do you remember, Phil, how much fun we had there?'

'I remember you always wanting just one more go, convinced you'd win, but we inevitably came out of there with less than we started,' Philip said, smiling. 'I won't be there to drag you away this time, so make sure you set yourself a limit.'

A little later, when Janie and Philip heard the front door open they both guessed it was Jessica returning. Instead they heard two voices in the hallway.

'Look who I bumped into on my way back from the bus stop,' Jessica said, dropping her scarf onto the settee. 'He was wandering about like a lost soul. I told him he should have come to the Pier with me. Maybe he'd have brought me good luck.'

'Don't tell me you lost again?' Philip said, laughing.

Janie watched as Luigi hovered in the doorway. 'It's okay, your father isn't here. He went back to the hotel a little while ago.'

Luigi shoulders relaxed a little.

'Luigi, why don't we go outside for a while. Into the garden?' Janie gestured to him to follow her through to the kitchen. Opening the back door, they made their way outside. Hedging ran around three sides of the small back garden, separating it from neighbours either side. At the far end, on the other side of the hedge, was a public footpath, used to access other houses in the street. Janie had avoided planting anything that needed too much careful tending. So most of the garden comprised a patch of lawn, with a small, paved seating area beside a solitary apple tree.

'See this,' she said, pointing to some marks on the trunk of the apple tree.

Luigi walked over to where she was standing and studied the tree trunk.

'I did that, when I was about eight or nine. I pinched dad's Swiss army knife. When Jessica found out I got into real trouble.'

'Because you damaged the tree?'

'Because I could have damaged myself,' she said, smiling at the memory. 'My dad has never seen it, of course, but he knows about it. When Jessica told him he came straight out here and ran his fingers over it and do you know what he said?'

'Did he tell you off?'

Janie ran her hand over the tree trunk. 'No, he told me I should have made a pretty picture instead of just scratches. *Remember,* he said, *if you're going to take risks make them worthwhile.*'

'What do you want me to say?' Luigi asked, a sharpness to his voice that was more than irritation.

'We only want to help you, but we can't unless you're completely honest with us. Did you go in to speak to Bertie the night he died?'

Luigi stared at Janie, his eyes narrowing as though she had slapped him around the face. Then he spoke. 'I wish I had never gone into his room that night. For so many reasons I wish I had never gone in. I wanted to confront him about his business dealings with my father.' Luigi paused as though he couldn't bear to voice the next words he uttered. 'If I'm arrested all I will see of England is the inside of a prison cell.' He clenched his hands into tight fists. 'I didn't do it, Janie. You know that, don't you?'

'You didn't kill him?'

'Do you think I'm capable of killing someone, when finding my mother like that nearly destroyed me?'

'Perhaps, if you were angry enough, if you felt Bertie was to blame somehow?'

'Why would I think he was to blame for my mother's death? I've already told you I lay that firmly on the shoulders of my father. And he knows it. I could see it in his face earlier.'

It was as though Janie had been handed a burning stick that she had to pass to Luigi with all the pain that would ensue. As they sat beneath the apple tree Luigi listened as Janie explained the truth about his mother's involvement with Bertie Williams. When she reached the end of the story she handed him the letter, but turned away as he read it. She waited for an explosion of anger, but instead Luigi started to cry, sobbing loudly, barely pausing to wipe his face or blow his nose. Throughout it all Janie sat quietly, wanting to wrap her arms around her aunt's Italian friend.

'I blamed my father, but all along it was my mother who had not committed to the marriage,' Luigi said, in a voice that was barely a whisper. 'It was Bertie she lost her heart to when she met him in the piazza that day. I had a crazy notion your dad might have been that soldier. I wish it had been him, or anyone else. Anyone but Bertie.'

Janie held her hand out in the direction of Luigi's voice. 'This is so difficult for you. It's news no-one wants to hear, but it was wartime, everything must have been so different from the life we know now.' Janie's tone was gentle, encouraging.

'He must have moved to Anzio so that he could get back in touch with her.' Luigi stood and paced backwards and forwards, staring at the ground as though there was something there that would help to make sense of the confusion in his mind.

'I suppose his business association with your father gave him the chance to see your mother.' Janie said, her voice tentative. 'And all those years, your father never guessed.'

Luigi took the handkerchief that was now wet through and folded it over, trying to find a dry part. 'I have hated my father for so long, but now it is myself I hate more. I was blind to the reason for my mother's unhappiness, perhaps if I'd known the truth I could have helped.'

'No, Luigi,' Janie said, her voice firmer now. 'You mustn't blame yourself. Bertie and your mother knew what they were doing. They must have realised the risks they were taking. A situation like that can only end up hurting everyone involved.'

Luigi looked at Janie, his eyes misting over again. 'You are right. It has hurt everyone.'

'And more recently?' Janie wanted to refer to Eloise's death, but couldn't find the right words. 'Do you think your mother feared your father finding out about her affair?'

Luigi shook his head. 'I don't know.'

'Your mother would never have considered divorce?'

'My mother was a practising Catholic. Her faith was important to her.'

'Perhaps Bertie tried to end the relationship, thinking he would save your mother any more pain?'

Luigi turned his back on Janie, putting his hands up to his head in a gesture of frantic emotion. 'She couldn't bear it, could she?' his voice was now so muffled with sobs that it was hard to decipher his words. 'She couldn't live without him, so she chose not to live. And that hurts more than anything. I wasn't enough for her to carry on living.'

Luigi crumpled down onto the ground, drawing his knees up and sinking his head onto them. Janie stood beside him, laid her hand on his back to try to comfort him.

After a while the sobbing stopped. It was as though he was on a train that had come to the end of its track. There was nowhere else to go, nothing else to say or do. He stood and brushed the damp strands of hair away from the side of his face. 'I need a cigarette.' He pulled the packet from his shirt pocket. Janie watched him as he lit it and took a long drag. 'And now comes the hard part,' he said, 'the apology I must make to my father. For years I have blamed him and now it seems he is blameless. I'm not sure I can find the words.'

Chapter 22

Thursday - Tidehaven Police Station

'I'm going back in to see DS Bright.' Janie moved Michelle from one arm to the other, putting the feeding bottle down on the kitchen table to focus on Greg.

'Are you hoping they'll have done the second post-mortem?'

'I want to do what I can to help Luigi move on with his life. He's had to deal with his mum dying and then he finds out that he never really knew her at all. It must be like losing her all over again.'

'It's really upset you, hasn't it?' Greg said, opening the bread bin and then closing it again. 'If I take these last slices for sandwiches you won't have any for your toast.'

'It's okay, I'll have cereal.'

'We need to be more organised.'

'You mean I need to be more organised.'

'You know there's no reason for the detective to tell you anything. It's not like you're family.'

'I'll have to use my persuasive powers then, won't I?'

'I need to go, but you know my thoughts. There's only so much you can do. It's not up to you to fix everything for everyone.' Greg sighed, running his hands through his hair. 'Long weekends are fine, but it just makes it harder to get back to 7am starts.'

'Michelle, your dad seems to forget that 7am is a lie-in for us.' Janie passed her to Greg, gently pushing his shoulder to ease him down into the chair. 'I'll make your sandwiches today, but don't get used to it,' she says, smiling.

'You're not taking Michelle into the police station, are you?'

'Frightened they'll arrest her?'

'Seriously, Janie. I don't like the idea of her being there. Take her round your dad's first, let Jessica keep an eye on her.'

As she approached the bland, concrete building housing the police station, Janie mulled over her options. In the past she had been able to hover in that space between interested member of the public and investigator. It would be good to know exactly what DS Bright thought of her. On occasions he had made it clear that he found her an irritation, but then there had been times over recent months when she detected a smidgen of admiration. She was certain that he respected her for her pursuit of the truth regarding Joel's death, even though he would never admit it. They crossed paths again when she was helping Hugh Furness, a case where she had more of a grasp of the situation than the detective did. This time the roles were reversed, but only up to a point. The police had information that she needed. And she had information that hopefully they would not need.

She waited while the desk sergeant rang through to Frank Bright's office. A few moments later he appeared, a flicker of something crossing his face before he resumed the blank expression he had mastered, that gave nothing away.

'Mrs Juke. You are here to see me?' The question was unnecessary, but she knew why he asked it. This was his domain, his rules and he was making that point clearly.

She followed him through to the interview room, where they had met just the day before. He waited while she took a seat on one side of the rough, wooden table. Then he pulled out a cigarette packet and placed it beside the already overfilled ashtray. Her mind went back momentarily to the first time she came into the police interview room, when she was pregnant with Michelle.

'This room could do with cheering up a little.' Janie waved her hands around, pointing at the bare walls.

'What did you have in mind? A few scenic views of Tidehaven Pier? Some fishing boats, a few sandcastles?' Frank Bright didn't try to hide the sarcasm in his voice. 'This is a police station, Mrs Juke, or had you forgotten that?'

'Of course not. It's just that you use the same room to interview the guilty, as well as the innocent. If you made the place a little more friendly people might feel more like opening up. It might help, in the long run.'

Frank took a cigarette from the packet, tapped the tip of it on the table, then held it in his fingers, unlit. 'And which are you?'

'Me?'

'Guilty or innocent?'

'I don't think you need to ask that, do you? I'm hardly likely to be guilty, am I?'

'Guilty of withholding information, perhaps?'

The detective put the cigarette down, removed a pencil from his pocket and licked the end of it, holding it poised over his notebook. Janie studied Frank Bright, using the pause in their conversation to revisit conversations she had had with Luigi.

'When you were here with Mr Denaro senior we spoke about the briefcase we'd found in Mr Williams' room,' Frank said.

'Yes, Luigi said it wasn't the one he lost. He was very disappointed.'

'Was he?'

The detective narrowed his eyes and laid down his pencil. A large envelope was laying on the table and now he slid it towards Janie.

'You want me to look inside?'

Frank watched as Janie opened the envelope, taking out several black and white photos. She laid them on the table and examined them. The photos were varying poses of a young couple. The woman was smartly dressed, always with a hat and the man wore a suit.

'Who are they?'

'I don't know. I thought you might know.'

'Where did you find the photos?'

'In the briefcase that Mr Denaro assures us is not his.'

In each of the photos the couple were gazing at each other in such a tender way it made Janie feel as though she was interrupting an intimate moment. Luigi had said his mother was pretty, but this woman was more than that. The photographer had caught the luminous quality of her skin, her high cheek bones and her gentle eyes. Eyes that couldn't hide the love she had for the man beside her. Many years had passed since the photos were taken, but Janie could still see the similarity between the man in the photos and the man who had lost his life on Good Friday evening.

Frank Bright had also noticed the likeness. It was one more thing that made him wonder. He watched Janie as she looked over the photos and tried to guess her thoughts. There was a link between the Denaros and Bertrand Williams, and these photos were relevant. But why?

'When your men searched Mr Williams' room. Did they find anything else of interest?' Janie's question brought his attention back to the present.

'Perhaps.'

'Now you're being coy with me, Detective Sergeant.'

'No, Mrs Juke. I'm merely reminding you that this is a police investigation.'

'Have you found something to link Luigi to the death of Mr Williams? Are you able to tell me anything? You have had your suspicions from the beginning, haven't you?'

He smiled and drew a long breath. 'You need to work on your observation skills, Mrs Juke.'

For the moment he had the upper hand and he was clearly enjoying it.

'You saw something in the room? Something that made you think someone else had been in there, besides Rosetta and me?'

He pushed his chair back and stood, picking the cigarette packet up from the table and putting it back in his pocket. Janie wondered whether his wife's concerns about his smoking were having an effect. She was sure that by now he would have had at least one cigarette, if not more.

'I'm guessing you've never smoked?' His question took her by surprise.

'No. Dad never smoked, nor did my aunt, so I suppose it wasn't something I grew up with. What about you? Have you smoked since you were a boy?'

'Mr Williams wasn't a cigarette smoker.'

Once again the direction of the conversation was bewildering. She watched the detective as he lent back against the wall and scuffed one foot across the floor.

Her mind raced through everything she had learned about Bertie Williams since his death, as she tried to determine the relevance of DS Bright's revelation.

'Come on now, Mrs Juke. Don't let me down. I have come to expect more of you than this.' He was playing with her now and the more he teased her, the more determined she was to reach the right conclusion before he handed it to her on a plate. 'Didn't you tell me you were an avid fan of Hercule Poirot?'

Janie took a deep breath and then forced her frown into a smile. 'He has taught me all I know.'

'You can be certain that Poirot wouldn't have missed this clue. He would have logged it in his notebook. You keep a notebook, don't you?'

She waited for him to make the next move.

'And I'm sure you have it with you today, in that bag of yours.'

Slipping her hand into her duffel bag, she drew out her notebook. She couldn't risk him seeing much of what she had written, particularly since her conversations with Luigi and his father. Instead, she opened it at the first page and laid it on the table, keeping her hand firmly on the cover.

'I'm guessing those are the first notes you made last Friday?'

'Yes. I jotted down a few things before I went to sleep that night. Everything I remembered from what I'd seen and heard.'

As she looked again at her notes, she replayed the events in her mind once more, conjuring up the scene. For a moment she closed her eyes to blot out Frank and the drab surroundings, replacing them with Bertie Williams' bedroom. Suddenly she saw it. The clue that

the detective had been referring to, the reason he had
been suspicious of Luigi from that first day. When she
opened her eyes DS Bright was sitting down again,
watching her with an amused expression on his face.

'You've seen it now, haven't you?'

'Yes. The ashtray.'

'Tell me how many cigarette stubs are in there.'

'Two?'

The detective tutted, a disappointed teacher whose
pupil had given the wrong answer. 'Three,' he said.

'And you think that...?'

'I don't think anything, Mrs Juke. Police work is all
about gathering evidence. A cigarette smoker had been
into Mr Williams' room that evening. Mrs Summer
doesn't smoke and on your admission, neither do you or
your family. I'm guessing your husband doesn't partake
of the dreaded weed, either?'

Janie shook her head.

'And Mr Williams is a pipe smoker. His pipe was left
on the dressing table with a pouch of pipe tobacco beside
it.'

'That just leaves one person. Mr Luigi Denaro. I
happen to know he likes his cigarettes almost as much as
I do. So, that ashtray tells me he not only went into Mr
Williams' room, but that he stayed long enough to smoke
three cigarettes. Now I ask myself one thing. Why
would a man lie? Why would he pretend he had not
entered the room, when it is evident that he did?'

Frank was right. Luigi had admitted going into
Bertie's room that evening but had said little about their
conversation. If Bertie had told Luigi about the affair
that would have been enough to get the Italian's temper
steaming. But Luigi appeared to be genuinely shocked

when she showed him the letter. Surely he was not so much of an actor that he could keep knowledge like that a secret.

One certainty was that if Frank Bright found out about the letter, and about the affair, he would have further reason to suspect Luigi. There was only one thing that would irrefutably prove Luigi's innocence.

'DS Bright,' she paused a moment to choose her words carefully. 'Have you received the results of the second post mortem?'

A slow smile crept across the detective's face. He stood and walked over to the back wall of the interview room, putting distance between himself and Janie. Then he turned and started to walk back towards the table again, with a purposeful but slow stride.

'And there we have it,' he said, watching for her reaction. 'You are hoping that if the demise of Mr Williams was the result of natural causes, then your friend Mr Denaro is off the hook.'

He paused, waiting for her to say something, but she remained silent. Then he continued. 'But that's where you're wrong.'

Janie shuffled in her chair, laying her hands out on the desk, appearing to examine her newly manicured fingernails. 'I am?' she said, looking back at the detective.

'I'm afraid so, yes.'

'Are you going to enlighten me?'

'I'm going to put you out of your misery. Mr Bertrand Williams died from heart failure, but Dr Filbert's initial thoughts were correct. Mr Williams was suffering from a serious lung condition. Meaning he would frequently have coughed up blood.' He kept his face as expressionless as possible and once again watched for her response.

'So there is no crime.' No question, just a definite statement.

'Perhaps.' Pulling out his packet of cigarettes, Frank lit one, turning away from Janie before exhaling. They both watched the circles of smoke dissipate as they reached the edge of the room.

'Are you playing games with me, Detective Sergeant?'

'A man has died, Mrs Juke, this is no time for games.' He flicked the cigarette ash into the ashtray and then continued. 'Let me paint you a picture. A young man goes into an older man's bedroom. They have an argument. The young man has a temper he struggles to control. The situation escalates, the conversation becomes heated. Perhaps the younger man pushes the older man, holds him by the shoulders, maybe even shakes him. The older man is in very poor health. He coughs up blood, he struggles to breathe. The young man does nothing to help him. What then, Mrs Juke? Do we have a victim and a criminal? Do we have a crime?'

When he finished speaking Frank rubbed his hands, as though he had put the finishing touches to a difficult crossword puzzle. Janie sat very still, still in her body, but not in her mind, as she revisited all she had learned about Luigi since his arrival a few days ago. She could imagine the hot-headed Luigi in Bertie's room. The blood spatter on Luigi's shirt could certainly have resulted from an argument, just as the detective had described. But Luigi was angry with his father, not with Bertie and in the short time she had known him she was certain Luigi wouldn't want to harm anyone. If there had been an argument Luigi would have had to keep that argument secret since the evening of Bertie's death. Luigi was sullen, yes, misguided even, but surely he couldn't be so devious as to keep such a dreadful secret.

'I've learned a lot from you, Detective Sergeant,' she said, smiling at him.

'You have?' Her statement took him by surprise and he returned the smile.

'You've always told me one thing is key. In fact, my mentor Poirot says much the same thing.'

'And what's that, Mrs Juke?'

'Evidence, Detective Sergeant. Without evidence there can be no conviction. What do some cigarette butts prove? I don't think we have a crime here, do you?'

Chapter 23

Friday - the Chandler household

When the phone rang the next morning, Philip hadn't expected to hear a policeman's voice at the other end of the line.

Luigi hadn't emerged from the little box room since Janie had shown him his mother's letter. He had spent most of the night sitting on the edge of his bed, the curtain pulled open so that he could look out into the black night. All the questions he had, that he knew could never be answered, spun round and round in his mind, like a long-playing record on repeat. His mother had loved a man she could never be with. Her beliefs, her sense of responsibility to her husband and her son, meant she would never have walked away from them to enjoy a life with another man. Instead, she had chosen a life of sadness, not only making herself unhappy, but denying happiness for everyone around her.

Luigi opened the window a little, the night air was chilly, but he was grateful for it. The more he thought about the dreadful waste, the more he struggled to breathe. He held onto the windowsill and took some deep gulps of air and then, as his breathing steadied he could feel the dam he had put on his emotions start to break. He closed the window, laid on the bed, pulled his knees up towards his chest and let the tears flow.

At some point during the early morning he must have dozed for a while. Then, as dawn broke, the light filled the room and woke him. In the bathroom he stared at his reflection in the mirror. His eyes were bloodshot, his hair damp around the edges of his face. He let the tap run and splashed his face with cold water, then ran his fingers through his hair. 'I need coffee,' he said to his reflection. 'Strong, hot and black.'

Philip heard Luigi come downstairs and make his way through to the kitchen. He recognised the distinctive smell of Italian coffee when Luigi filled the percolator.

'Morning,' Philip said, choosing his greeting with care. 'Did you sleep?'

Luigi shook his head, momentarily forgetting Philip's blindness. 'I think I dozed a little,' he said, surprised by the croakiness in his voice. It was as though he had spent hours screaming and shouting, instead all the noise had been inside his head.

'Coffee is an excellent idea. If there's enough I'll join you.'

When the percolator started to bubble, Luigi turned the gas off and waited for the coffee to settle before filling two of the smallest cups he could find in one of the kitchen cupboards. 'You need some Italian coffee cups,' he said. 'These are fine for tea, but good Italian coffee...'

'I know, it should be drunk strong, hot and black,' Philip said, the beginnings of a smile on his face.

They sat in silence for a while. Luigi studied Philip, noticing how accurately he was able to locate the cup, bringing it to his lips with no hesitation.

'I've had a long time to learn,' Philip said, sensing the Italian's inquisitiveness.

'You must have had to start again, with everything.'

Philip smiled. 'I've still got my memories. Nothing can take those away.'

'But not all memories are good.'

'I could choose to replay the accident, those first few

months when I knew I would never see my daughter's face again. Instead I've chosen to let them go. I lost my sight, not my life. Hanging on to the bad times can only destroy the good times to come. And they will come, in the end.'

'I can't imagine good times.'

'That's because it's not the end, not yet.'

Luigi stood and moved the empty cups to the draining board.

'I had a phone call this morning, from the police,' Philip said.

'What do they want now?'

'They've asked you to call back into the station.'

Philip heard Luigi mutter something under his breath. 'Do you want Janie to go with you?'

'Thank you, no. I'm ready for whatever they want to accuse me of. I have done nothing wrong, so I need to trust your British justice.'

Standing outside the police station, Luigi took some deep breaths. His heart was beating uncomfortably fast. Even smoking a cigarette didn't seem to help.

He gave his name to the desk sergeant who asked him to wait. A few moments later DS Bright appeared, with a large plastic bag in his hand.

'Shall we go through to the interview room, Mr Denaro.'

Once inside Frank Bright asked Luigi to take a seat. As he sat he immediately lit a cigarette and the detective slid the ashtray towards him. Luigi nodded his thanks.

'I have some news for you,' Frank said. It was as if he was playing with Luigi, waiting for a reaction. 'You'll be pleased to know that your briefcase has been found.' He opened the plastic bag and removed the briefcase with a flourish, placing it on the table. Then he watched as Luigi took the key from his breast pocket and unlocked the case. He put his hand inside the main compartment and felt for the envelope he prayed would still be there.

'I am very grateful,' he said, standing and tucking the case under his arm.

'Not so fast. Don't you want to know how it came to be returned? And aren't you going to show me what's inside?'

'I told you before, the items are personal. I am very relieved to have it back in my possession and now I would like to leave.'

'It's a good job there was a luggage ticket on it. That and the detailed report you gave to the French police helped to bring matters to a happy conclusion. Whatever is in the briefcase must be very important to you.'

Luigi remained standing, removed the envelope and slid his hand inside to take out the contents, which he then spread across the table.

'My mother,' he said, running a finger lightly over each of the black and white photos.

'Ah,' Frank Bright said, alternating his gaze to look first at the photos and then at Luigi. 'She is a striking looking woman.'

'Was. She is no longer. My mother is dead and these photos are all I have left of her. Now you can see why I was so desperate to retrieve them.'

Frank returned his gaze to the photos. He had seen this woman's face recently, in another set of photos, the ones he removed from Mr Williams' briefcase.

'Did your mother know Mr Williams?'

'Of course. Bertie was a business associate of my

father. They all mixed in the same circles. Now, unless you have any more questions for me I would like to leave.'

'I have something else for you before you leave.' Frank put his hand into his jacket pocket. 'Your passport, Mr Denaro.'

'I am no longer a suspect?'

'I no longer have a crime to investigate. We now know Mr Williams died of natural causes.' Luigi took the passport from the detective's hand, but Frank Bright retained a grip on it. For a few moments each had a hand on the passport as they held each other's gaze. 'When there is no crime I don't need a suspect, but that doesn't mean I don't still have my suspicions about you, Mr Denaro.'

'You are a policeman. Being suspicious is part of your job.'

Frank released his hold on the passport. 'I know you went into his room that night. But I'd like to hear you say it.'

'As you say, Detective Sergeant, there is no longer any crime to investigate. So, thank you for my passport and my briefcase and now I'll be on my way.'

Chapter 24

Friday - the Royal Elizabeth Hotel

Just one week had passed since a man's death in the otherwise sleepy town of Tamarisk Bay. In that one week life had changed irrevocably for Luigi and Alberto Denaro. What they thought they knew about the woman at the centre of their lives now needed to be looked at again with fresh eyes. It was like breaking apart a jigsaw puzzle and trying to form a new image. An almost impossible task.

The Chandler family had offered kindness and understanding and Alberto had been thinking about one way to repay that kindness.

Down at the hotel reception he asked if he could make an international phone call. A few minutes later he was connected to the Dutti household.

'Signora Dutti, it's Alberto Denaro, can I speak with your husband?'

The hotel receptionist pretended to be engrossed in the guest register, while straining to listen to the attractive lilt of an Italian voice. She couldn't understand a word he was saying, except every now and then he said, *Si, si.* She knew enough to know that he was saying *yes.* She had wanted to learn Italian for ages. Maybe this was her chance. Perhaps she should ask this man if he knew of any other Italians in Tamarisk Bay who would give her a few lessons.

The telephone conversation came to an end and the Italian was standing at the reception desk once more.

'You can put the charge on my bill?'

'Yes sir, *si,*' she said, giggling at the thought that she had been brave enough to try out her newly acquired vocabulary with a native speaker. But Mr Denaro was barely aware of her attempts at Italian. He had other things on his mind. The conversation with Signor Dutti had confirmed his suspicions and now he needed to speak to Jessica.

He made his way along the seafront to Philip's house. Before he had a chance to ring the doorbell the door opened. Jessica almost bumped into him as she stepped out, her gaze focused on buttoning her jacket.

'Oh, Signor Denaro, sorry.'

'May I speak with you?' he said.

'I was just going out. Would you like to walk with me?'

He turned to follow her along the path.

'I'm so sorry about your friend. It must have been a dreadful shock for you,' she said.

He stayed one step behind her and took a breath, causing her to turn. The words he wanted to say were slippery, eager to escape like fish from a net.

'You worked for Signor Dutti?'

She stopped walking for a moment, surprised by the direction of the conversation.

'I know the Dutti family,' he said.

'Ah, yes, of course.' Her thoughts went to the two children. The image of their bright faces made her smile.

'Signora Chandler, I'm afraid I may have had something to do with you losing your job.'

Still the connections in his story remained elusive.

'Let me explain,' he said.

'Yes, that would be helpful.'

They had reached the bus stop at the end of Philip's

road. She gestured to Alberto to sit beside her in the wooden shelter.

'You know that I am in business? From time to time my business dealings overlapped with Signor Dutti. It is useful to have a network to support one another.' He turned to look at her, as if wanting reassurance. 'I'm sure you understand?'

Jessica nodded.

'But Aldo Dutti has also become a friend. He wanted to help. Now he realises he may have made a mistake.'

'What sort of mistake?'

'He wanted to help with a family matter. That is where he may have, how should I say, stepped over the mark.'

He approached his explanation as though he was laying out a complicated scientific formula, with many equations leading to the final conclusion.

'Aldo knew that there had been a rift between me and my son. But he did not know the reason for the argument.'

Jessica hesitated before speaking. 'Did he know your wife had died?'

'Yes. But he knew nothing else. Not about the manner of my wife's death, or ...' He stood and took a few paces along the path, turning on his heel and returning to stand in front of her. 'When he saw that you had befriended my son, he thought perhaps you were the cause of the rift.'

'I don't understand, why would I want to create difficulties between you and your son.'

He sighed. 'No, I am not explaining myself. Aldo and I, we are old-fashioned in our thinking. You are older than my son. Aldo thought I would disapprove.'

'I don't know what to feel more annoyed about. Your friend judging my character, or you assuming that your son and I are in an inappropriate relationship.'

'I have offended you and that is not my intention.' He clasped his hands together. 'My son is an adult. He is free to make his own choices.'

'Signor Denaro, Luigi and I are just friends. In fact, we aren't much more than acquaintances. Believe me when I tell you that I am not looking for a romantic relationship, but if I was then age would not come into the equation.'

'Please accept my apologies. I am sure you can see that I have made many mistakes in my life as a result of not understanding what makes for a lasting relationship. Perhaps if I opened my eyes and my mind then Eloise would not have looked elsewhere for love and companionship.'

Before returning to the hotel there was one more person he wanted to extend his hand in friendship to. When Rosetta answered the door and found Alberto on her doorstep she tutted, but stood back to let him in.

'I am sorry I had to ask your son to leave, but this has been a difficult time for me.'

'I understand and please don't apologise.' He stood in the hallway, feeling a little awkward. He had spent a lifetime avoiding emotional conversations, but perhaps now, after all that had happened, this was the right time to learn. 'I am sure you are busy, but if you have a moment to talk?'

'We will have some coffee together, come into the kitchen.'

He sat, watching her as she busied herself with making

coffee. Then, while they waited for the coffee to percolate, he said, 'You have lived in England a long time. It must feel like home to you.'

'Italy is my home.'

'And you have family there still?'

'My parents are in heaven, but, yes I have a brother and sister, some nieces and nephews.'

'You don't ever think of returning?'

She poured the coffee and took a sip of coffee, the beginnings of a smile around the edges of her mouth. 'I think about it all the time. And now, with you and your son here, it made Italy seem close again, and at the same moment even further away.'

'I understand. Mrs Summer, I would like to make a suggestion, but I don't want to offend you.'

She moved the empty coffee cups to the sink, running hot water into them, but leaving them in the bowl and returned to sit opposite Alberto.

'I have spent much of my life creating a successful business. The money I have made means I can live a comfortable existence, I can take pleasure in a lovely home, a smart car, fine wines. Money has its uses, but I have used it poorly. Now I would like to start using it for good.'

Rosetta didn't really understand what Alberto was trying to say, but she realised he needed to say it.

'I would like to pay for your flight to Italy. It would be a chance for you to see your family.'

'Why? You don't know me, you don't know my family.'

'We are both Italians. I would like to think we could be friends and friends help each other. Perhaps you could visit me in Anzio while you are over. I would be very happy to show you around.'

It was rare for Rosetta to struggle for words. They usually came tripping out of her mouth, often before she had prepared them. But now all she could do was to take Alberto's hand in hers and whisper, '*Grazie.*'

A little later that day, when Luigi arrived at the Royal Elizabeth Hotel, his father was waiting for him in the foyer. Alberto was mulling over his conversation with Jessica and wondering if it wouldn't have been better for him to say nothing about Aldo's mistaken assumptions. Rather than calming waters he seemed to have only muddied them. But as soon as he saw his son walking towards him with a briefcase tucked under his arm, all thoughts of Jessica and the Duttis vanished.

'You've found it,' he said, rushing forwards to put his arm around his son's shoulder.

Luigi stepped back, still uncomfortable with the thought of close contact with the man who had been on the edges of his life for so long. 'Yes, it was handed in to the police. I don't know who took it, I don't much care. I have it back, that's all that matters.'

They moved over to two empty armchairs in one corner of the lounge. Alberto ordered two glasses of orange juice from the hotel bar, which a waiter brought over, taking his time to set them down on the low glass table. Alberto took a small leather change purse from his jacket pocket and gave the waiter a shilling.

Luigi opened the briefcase, taking out the photos and laying them on the glass table. He heard his father take a sharp breath at the sight of his wife. The woman who had stayed with him for so many years when all the time she loved another man. Not just any man, but his good

207

friend, Bertie.

Luigi watched his father as he gently touched each photo.

'Did you never suspect? All those years and there was nothing that made you suspicious?'

'I was always looking in the wrong places.' Alberto picked up one of the photos and brought it to his lips.

'Do you hate him for what he did?'

'Bertie? No, I don't hate him. Blaming him, blaming your mother, none of it will make a difference now. I made mistakes as well, always busy, not understanding what was really important. She was my wife and I loved her. Nothing can change that.'

'What will happen to Bertie's business?' Luigi said.

'He has a sister, I suppose it will all go to her. She lives here in England. Perhaps we can go together to visit her?' Alberto took a sip of his orange juice, moving the glass around a little, listening to the ice cubes clink against each other.

'Perhaps.' Luigi shifted in his seat, looking around the lounge before he continued. 'Do you want the truth?'

'Don't I already have the truth?'

'Not all of it, no.'

'If there is anything you want to share with me now, then, yes, I am happy to hear it.'

'There is still a part of you that thinks I am guilty, isn't there? That I did something to Bertie to cause his death.'

'You are my son and I love you. Nothing can change that.'

'I told you before that I went into Bertie's room that night and I spoke to him. Bertie was not a well man. While I was with him he had a terrible coughing fit. There was blood. I tried to help him, I sat on the bed

208

beside him, waited until he could breathe more comfortably. I got blood on my hands, on my shirt. It was only later, when I knew he had died that I could see how it looked.'

'You could have come to me, told me the truth. We could have explained to the police.'

Luigi shook his head. 'Rosetta knows how it can be with the police. You are innocent and they make you feel guilty.'

Alberto finished his drink, setting the glass down on the table. He went to put his hand out towards his son, but then drew it back again.

'Were you able to talk with Bertie, once he recovered?'

'I told him how angry I was with you. In fact, we laughed about it.'

'You laughed?'

'He said he had always wished for a son like me, that if things were different he would love to teach me about his business. I could have been his apprentice, he said. That's when I laughed. I told him that I would make the worst apprentice.'

'And what did Bertie say?'

'That my mother had been so proud of me. I thought it was a strange thing to say. And that's when he laughed. *Life is strange,* he said.' Luigi closed his eyes, picturing the last time he saw Bertie. 'He was fine when I left him. *I'll rest a moment,* he said, *and then I'll join you downstairs.* If I'd stayed with him a bit longer...who knows, perhaps I could have helped him, called someone.'

Alberto ran his finger around the edge of his empty glass. 'You couldn't have known. We can all say *what if.* I have made many mistakes in my life, but perhaps now is the time to start on a new road.'

'Janie has a friend who might help us to find out more about *mamma,*' Luigi said, glancing sideways at his father. 'I'd like to speak to her. But perhaps you want to go back home. You have your business affairs to deal with.'

'We will speak to the friend together. If we can walk in your mother's footsteps, perhaps we can tread some new paths, ones that will help to heal all that has been broken.' He slid his hand across the table towards his son.

'I'd like that,' Luigi said.

While the Denaros were exploring ways to connect after years of misunderstanding, another family in Tamarisk Bay were connecting in an entirely different way.

Greg laid Michelle down in her cot, setting Barnaby bear down beside her and tucking the blanket up around them both. He stood for a while, gazing down at his daughter, who didn't seem entirely happy with the idea that it was time to sleep.

'Now there's a picture, stay just as you are and I'll grab my camera,' Janie said, standing in the bedroom doorway.

'She needs to go to sleep and she won't all the time I'm standing here.'

Janie moved to stand next to her husband and wrapped her arm around his waist. 'We're so lucky, aren't we? Imagine what it must be like to live most of your life loving someone you can't be with.'

'Good job I wasn't already snapped up when we first met.'

'You are so cheeky. And now we've got this little darling. She might have her own share of heartache one day and we'll have to stand by and watch.'

'The first person to break my daughter's heart, will get

his nose broken, at the very least.'

'That's fighting talk, Mr Juke. Do you hear that, Michelle, your dad is going to be vetting anyone who so much as glances your way.'

'Ah, finally, I win the bet. Did you see that, she just smiled at me.'

'I think you'll find that was a touch of wind.'

'Michelle, your mother knows nothing. Calls herself a private investigator and misses the most obvious clue of all.'

Janie studied her daughter's face and then turned to look at Greg.

'What clue?'

'That dimple in her chin, see the way it moved just now when she smiled.'

'Okay, you win. What's the prize, anyway?'

'A quiet night in with my wife, with no talk of crimes or mysteries.'

'Done,' she said, laying her head down on his shoulder. 'I'm sure I can manage one night.'

Thank you

As part of my research for the series I contacted The Keep, which provides a wonderful archive of East Sussex records: **www.thekeep.info/collections/** They helped to ensure the details about Janie's library van was as accurate as possible. Sussex Police were able to confirm the back story for Janie's father, Philip, all made sense.

It was wonderful to have a chance to share a few of my childhood memories of Italy, especially that wonderful train journey from Rome to Calais, which I did many times with my family. But to get a glimpse into what life must have been like in Anzio during 1944 I was lucky enough to have the help of my cousin Anna and her grandchildren Nicole and Riccardo, as well as another cousin, Loredana, and several good friends.

Most authors will agree that writing can be a lonely pursuit. So I consider myself very fortunate to have the encouragement and support of some wonderful people. Janie might have withered along the way if it were not for them. My brilliant writing buddies, Chris and Sarah, and my brother, David, continue to offer me not only invaluable critiques, but inspiration to keep going. Heartfelt thanks also go to family and friends too numerous to list here. I am grateful to you all.

And, in the words of one of my favourite songs, my love and thanks go to my husband Al, who is *'the wind beneath my wings'*.

If this was your first Janie Juke mystery, you might like to take a look at the other books in the Sussex Crime series:

The Tapestry Bag
Lost Property

Available from...

Amazon.com
Amazon.co.uk
Amazon.ca
Amazon.com.au